DIARY OF A MALAYALI MADMAN

diary of a
malayali madman

N. PRABHAKARAN

Translated by Jayasree Kalathil

DEEP VELLUM PUBLISHING

DALLAS, TEXAS

Deep Vellum Publishing
3000 Commerce St., Dallas, Texas 75226
deepvellum.org · @deepvellum

Deep Vellum is a 501c3 nonprofit literary arts organization
founded in 2013 with the mission to bring
the world into conversation through literature.

First published in India in 2019 by Harper Perennial
An Imprint of HarperCollins Publishers
A-75, Sector 57, Noida, Uttar Pradesh 201301, India
www.harpercollins.co.in

First US Edition, 2023

Support for this publication was provided in part by grants from the
National Endowment for the Arts, Amazon Literary Partnership, the Texas
Commission on the Arts, City of Dallas Office of Arts & Culture, and the
George & Fay Young Foundation.

THE
GEORGE & FAY YOUNG
FOUNDATION

LIBRARY OF CONGRESS CONTROL NUMBER: 2022945443

ISBN: 978-1-64605-207-3 (paperback)
ISBN: 978-1-64605-233-2 (ebook)

Typeset in 11/15 Arno Pro

Cover design by Emily Mahon

Interior layout and typesetting by KGT

PRINTED IN CANADA

Contents

wild goat

1.

No one sees him; no one hears him. No one, perhaps, even knows about him. High up on the cliff, at the edge of the frightening drop, he is alone in the moonlight, a forlorn slice of darkness, a dream animal. He bleats. His gaze wanders the valley. In the countless lanes hidden beneath the undergrowth, he searches for me. Agitated wanderings, secret pleasures sprouting like new meadow grass, anxious thickets of thorn—his memories are endless. He waits for the moment when they will merge together in a brilliant dance, a moment like a drop of fire. In the intensity of his anticipation, he calls out, again and again.

2.

Tomorrow morning, they will wake me up and take me to the city. The jeep is already parked in the yard, and Pappachan is asleep on a mat on the veranda. He will wake up before dawn, wash the jeep, bathe and have his breakfast. He will cross himself and sit behind the wheel, start the jeep and bring it to life. It will crawl up the hill before racing down in a cloud of red dust.

Riding shotgun will be Babychayan. Pailychettan will sit in the back with me, holding on to my arm and never taking his eyes off me.

They'll take me to the doctor. Leaving me outside, Babychayan will tell the doctor all about me, half of which will be lies. The doctor will know this. Still, he'll call me inside, sit me down in a revolving chair and interrogate me. My answers will also be half-truths and lies. Then they will make me lie down on a high bed and look, kindly, into my eyes. And after that? Injections that will send me into the tender world of forgetfulness. ECT. Chains. Solitary confinement meant for dangerous patients. Actually, no, I don't know, I have no idea what fate awaits me.

3.

Last year, on my way home for the Christmas holidays, I had an idea. I wanted to forget everything that I had learnt, and make sure that I didn't learn anything new from then on. I didn't spend time analysing why I had this idea. In fact, I was not able to analyse it as it had already taken root inside me and overwhelmed me.

After the holidays, I went back to college, attended my classes, even took part in a play on College Day, performing the part of an old migrant man.

After the last exam, everyone left and the hostel was deserted. I stayed on for one more night and then set out for home early in the morning. The bus was more crowded than usual. It was almost noon by the time the bus gasped its way up the hill roads and stopped in front of No. 1 Toddy Shop.

As I walked home through the cashew orchard, I made up a game: recite all the words I remembered one by one and spit them out.

The sun-baked lanes were deserted, an uncomfortable silence waited for me around each corner like a rasping sigh.

I began the game.

Sublimity. Objective correlative. Syllable. Diphthong. Absurdism. So many words, so many concepts.

By the time I was walking down the hill, my mouth was dry and my throat sore. I stopped the game. A thick fog of silence spread inside and around me, and followed me all the way home.

I lingered in the front yard for a while before ringing the doorbell.

Anniechechi opened the door and, with the usual, 'Hi Georgootty,' she walked back, calling casually upstairs, 'Georgootty is here.'

Babychayan was busy, his table covered in envelopes and pieces of paper. He handed me a file with a list of addresses and said: 'Georgootty, write these addresses on these envelopes. I need a shower.'

I washed my face and hands, hung my shirt on the clothes-line and carefully picked up the pen. I'd finished writing the addresses on around twenty-five envelopes by the time Babychayan came back. Casually, he picked up an envelope and I saw his face blanch. 'Georgootty!' he thundered.

I looked at him and was not afraid. I gave him a slow smile. He stared at me and, as I continued smiling, something like fear congealed in his wide open eyes. I had written my address on all of the envelopes.

4.

Anniechechi and I are of the same age, but she is very confident—arrogant even. Her arms are as strong as any man's. Her substantial body radiates an energy that diminishes everything around her. Her eyes reflect poise and competence.

She rules over this household. That's not surprising, really, as there is no one else here to be the ruler apart from them—my brother Baby and his wife Annie. My duty is to obey them.

5.

Last year, on the day before Easter, our father passed away. Appachan had been drinking all day long. In the evening, he pigged out on beef, drank some more and went to bed. A little after midnight, he got up and vomited—not what he ate and drank, but a massive amount of blood. Then he keeled over and died, face down in that blood. The neighbours came first; they informed the priest. One by one, the whole community was there, crowding over the yard, veranda and the entire compound.

The deceased—Varkichettan—was a man of consequence in our community. He'd migrated from Manimala at the age of forty-five, his only companion a young woman. It was he who paved the way for others from Ponkunnam, Kanjirappally, Ranni and so on, other migrants who made this forest their home.

Hillsides that barely let in sunlight, ebony-skinned people, meadows where tigers skulked. Varkichettan, my father, fought the forest, the animals and the forest folk single-handedly, cultivated plants and trees strange to the hills, and created a thirty-acre rubber plantation. He was the first to step up to build roads, the church and the school. He fathered five children. The fifth childbirth took his wife's life and, with that, he lost his vigour and his drive, and succumbed to a life steeped in alcohol and ganja.

All of his five children were boys. The eldest two didn't make it past their infancy. The middle son, Kunjukunju, wasted away his life drinking and whoring around until someone beat him to death. That left the last two: Baby and Georgekutty. People pointed at us and said, 'That young one, Georgekutty – he is feckless. Won't come to anything. But his brother Baby – he is a chip off the old block.'

6.

The task of analysing and differentiating between good and bad has always been beyond my capabilities. However, there is one thing I do know, and it is this: Love is a want, a privation. One can love another person only as long as that person is in some way or the other inferior to oneself. Otherwise, it becomes either a kind of uneasy dependency or a need for control disguised as affection. Anything else is just a fantasy. The only reason people enact friendship or closeness to one another is to overcome some sense of deficiency within them.

Maybe these thoughts are just a reflection of the times I live in, a world view restricted by my current context. I would much rather not have any thoughts at all about the human condition, and get through life—like an ant or a musk deer—concerned only with the day-to-day needs of my small world, but I seem to be unable to do that. Even my own experiences seem beyond me.

It is Babychayan who takes care of all my needs, makes decisions about every aspect of my life—the food I eat, the clothes I wear, where I go . . . I am in need of nothing, never had to wait for anything.

'Georgootty, you have everything,' Govindankutty, who is now dead, had said to me several times. His family were the rulers of this place once. It was from his ancestor that my father bought this land, paying six rupees for an acre. This whole hill belonged to Govindankutty's family at one point but, by the time he was born, all that was left was the family home and the bit of land it sat on.

Govindankutty knew privation, not having enough money for his favourite food, for clothes, for love . . . And he died stuck in privation. Imprisoned within that frail body, his heart simply stopped beating one day.

I do not love death; I don't want it to come slyly, uninvited, and steal me away. I will not allow God to humiliate me in that way.

7.

I was sitting behind Appayi's hut, eating sweet potato. Dusk settled around us, the shadows under the jackfruit tree darkened. The dying embers of Appayi's fire warmed us and cast a dull red glow on our skins.

Appayi handed me a strip of banana leaf with a chunk of steaming, peeled sweet potato on it. He added a piece of jaggery to intensify its sweetness, and smiled at me like a naughty child. He ate all his food, even meat, cooked like this—directly on an open fire.

Like most of the migrants here, Appayi was originally from

Thiruvithamkur. He came up here with his wife almost thirty years ago. While the other migrants took root and put out new shoots, Appayi withered and dried. With no children to nurture and no relatives to keep them company, all he and his wife Sarachettathi had to show for those hard years was a hut and the ten cents of land on which it stood.

Appayi was over fifty, his hair and beard were completely grey. His eyes were silver from long, endless days of sleeplessness. Exhaustion darkened the wrinkles on his face. Tethered to his barren life, his wife too had become a lifeless old wraith.

'Let's go into the forest tomorrow,' I said, gripped by a sudden desire. He nodded idly.

Appayi was the king of the forest. He knew it like the lines in his palm. For thirty years, he had lived off it, trusting in it and refusing to plant rubber, sell cashew or work for other planters. He was born for the forest. His skin exuded the scent of dry leaves soaked in dew. He was good at avoiding the forest guards when he went into the forest to cut rattan canes. He wove them into baskets and his wife sold them at the market.

Appayi had no worries, no anxieties about tomorrow, not even about death. He spent days on end in the forest. No one knew how he survived in there. In the forest, Appayi had no enemies.

Still, on that evening, in the light of the dying fire, I saw that his face was darker than usual. I heard him whisper the name of the Christ between mouthfuls. His voice was shaky. Something was troubling him but I didn't want to ask him about it. So I sat there, silently sharing his anxiety.

'Appayi ... Hey, Appayi ...'

An anxious voice called out from the front of the hut. I recognized the voice instantly. Babychayan!

As he got up and walked to the front of the hut, Appayi gave me a stern look telling me to stay put. I stood back and watched them whisper before setting off together.

When they disappeared down the lane, Sarachettathi came out of the hut.

'Looks like she is gone,' she said.

'Who?'

'Rosily. Pathrose's daughter.'

I had no idea what she was talking about. Seeing my bewilderment, she said, 'Your brother knocked her up. They gave her some medicine to get rid of it. Seems like it has all gone wrong now.'

She stopped speaking and looked around, scared.

8.

'Anniechechi, who are you scared of?' The question popped out of my mouth, unchecked. She was sitting across from me at the dining table, just the two of us. Babychayan had gone out.

She stared at me, not quite sure what to make of my question. Then I saw her face darken, little by little, as the question spun around in her brain and she came to an unintended conclusion.

An oceanic tiredness washed over me. I noticed that my voice was trembling and realized that I myself was not completely sure what my question meant.

'None of us are really alive, chechi,' I said, anxiously. 'Every night, the moon fills our yard with light too, but none of us see it. We are too busy to appreciate it.'

Anniechechi stared at me and, consumed by a desire to subjugate the sense of superiority implicit in her look, I persevered: 'Take coffee, for instance. We drink our coffee. Babychayan runs around buying more and more acres of coffee plantations. You've seen coffee bushes, haven't you? There's purity in their shadows, a sacredness you cannot find even in the church.

'Or take Mathan, the man who works in our orchards,' I continued. 'He might be a simpleton but he is still a human being. We don't acknowledge that, do we? Or consider the deer and the rabbits. The weather cools down and we pull on our sweaters, huddle under our blankets. But the rabbit and the deer—they run around in the forest, in the plantations, frolicking in the cold. Or the whistling wind that rises in the afternoon. Do we hear its music? We don't, because we sit in here, behind closed doors and windows.

'You'll soon have children. Would they be any better, have any appreciation for any of this? My father settled in these hills, cultivated rubber, made a whole heap of money, and we live in splendour because of it. There are others who've succumbed to a life of drunkenness and debauchery and violence, but not us! My brother is a smart man, a strong and capable man. He knows how to make money and he'll become an even richer man than my father. We Punnakkunnel folk are at the top, what with our rubber and cardamom and black pepper, and our own jeep. We'll acquire more land, expand this house even further. Still, chechi, how can we go on worshipping God and Mammon at the same time? I don't know. I want to say . . . Have you looked east from our rooftop, chechi? The forest is right there, within grasping distance and, beyond that, the forests of Mysore. So many trees . . . So green, so achingly green that even the colour seems alive. And I feel like crying. All these trees . . . All these forests . . .'

'Georgootty, stop it,' Anniechechi interrupted in a stern voice. She was on her feet. Her nose was red, and I saw the flames of anger flickering in her eyes.

But I was not afraid. I did not feel I had said anything inappropriate.

9.

In the evening as the light faded, Babychayan came home with a group of people. They sat on the veranda and talked loudly. I had no interest in their conversation, but I could hear what they were saying.

'We have to grab the seat this time and not let go. If Babychayan steps forward, there is no reason why we can't win. If they won't give it to us, we'll take it anyway—by force if necessary.'

Someone laughed loudly. The ruckus continued, steadily increasing in volume as the drinking and card-playing carried on late into the night. Much later, they left and silence descended upon the house.

I lay in my bed, sleepless, watching the moonlight through the open window. Gradually, an image took shape in my mind, an image of an owl, resplendent with silvery feathers and round eyes overflowing with a timeless wisdom. I watched carefully as the owl pulsated, alternately growing as large as the sky and shrinking into a tiny dot.

A knock on the door brought me back from this spectacle. I got up and opened the door to find my brother standing there, swaying on unsteady legs.

He grabbed me by my collar, and shouted: 'So you've started smoking ganja now, have you?'

He paid no attention to my denial and slapped me across the face. I tried to get away from him, but he punched me in the stomach and pushed me on to the bed. I watched his body grow big and terrifying right before my eyes. I couldn't breathe.

10.

Anniechechi's father was a businessman in Bangalore, an ogre with slabs of fat hanging off his cheeks and jowls, and thick, black hair covering his forearms. His thighs were hunks of meat struggling to burst out of his trouser legs, his pale tongue slipped out every now and then to slither over his lips. But the most disgusting thing about him was his voice—the baying of a greedy, hankering animal.

We didn't have a relationship that called for strong emotions, love or hate. Still, I felt a deep-seated hatred for him from the very first time I met him, a hatred that only intensified every time I saw him after that. I was certain that he saw me as an enemy, and that every word from his mouth was a poisonous dart.

Anniechechi was his only daughter and he came to see her often, laden with presents. He would hug and kiss her on her forehead and talk non-stop. In the presence of her doting father, Anniechechi changed into someone else, and the house reverberated with her happy laughter and conversation.

On his visit last month, he asked, 'Annie, dear, how is Georgootty doing?'

'How's he doing? As always. No change.'

'Aren't you scared of him?'

'I used to be, at first. But he is harmless.'

'Still. It must be hard to have a sick person living with you ...'

'Sick? Do you know what he says? He says everyone else is sick.'

Anniechechi guffawed and her father laughed with her.

'That's not surprising, is it? What else would a mad person say?' he said and laughed again.

Like a cold wind carrying the stench of decay, his laughter hung heavily in my room.

11.

The fever has let up its assault on my body. I am drenched in sweat. A dry wind swirls in my head.

I don't know how long I had been lying in my bed, shivering, hugging myself under the blanket. But now, in the blessed relief of sweat, a gratifying tiredness takes hold of my body. It is peaceful, death-like.

My body is as light as a piece of cotton soaring away to great heights, caught in the lightest breeze. But my heart? It has grown as wide as the earth, as high as the sky. It encompasses all living creatures—plants and trees, birds and beasts, and the millions of human beings ruling over all of them. The plants grow, the trees flower and fruit. Unaware of the changes around them, the birds and the beasts wander through the meadows and the forests, mate, reproduce and, fearful and submissive, live out their lives acquiescing to man's supremacy, while he hunts and copulates and continues the relentless pursuit of greatness. Within and outside the borders of his own creation, he battles with his fellow men. The acrid smell of smoke and the screams suffuse my heart.

I look up at the sky. Its arched ceiling pulls closer, bringing the sun, the moon and the stars nearer. I am enclosed by cooling clouds, enveloped in their gentle damp fragrance. The earth and the sky embrace me in their vast love.

Oh God, I can't take it any more. This love, this bliss, the well of strange emotions springing inside me . . . Oh God, oh God, I cannot bear this any more.

12.

Annammachi was over fifty years old and had been our maid servant for almost twenty years. People said she was also my father's mistress. After Appachan died and the household came under Babychayan's control, she had to leave—Babychayan threw her out.

My mother died when I was born, and Appachan handed me over to Annammachi. Her daughter, Cecily, was about a year and a half old. Cecily and I grew up at her breast; she loved and cared for us equally.

Cecily and I studied in the same school until class five when she dropped out. At first, she stayed at home doing nothing. Then she went to tailoring classes for a while, before going to work, like many others, as a daily wage labourer.

It was Annammachi who took care of all my needs until I was big enough to look after myself. On the day I left for college, she hugged me and sobbed. I was going to the city far away, she said, and should be careful not to let myself fall into its bad ways.

Annammachi's house stood in the shadow of a cluster of rocks on the other side of the stream running on the north boundary of our land. Each time I came home for holidays, I escaped from my own house and ran to hers at the first opportunity. How long had it been since I visited her? At least four or five years.

It was afternoon when I walked into her yard. Cecily was lying face down on a mat on the veranda and scrambled up on hearing my footsteps.

'Oh it's you, Georgootty. Christ, you scared me!' she said, pressing her palm on her chest. There was an unfamiliar edge to her voice. 'Ammachi is not in.'

'Where is she?'

'Didn't you hear? She has a new job now,' Cecily said, laughing. 'Cooking upma at the school. She won't be back until evening.'

I wasn't sure what to say. Cecily continued, 'Appachan is also not in. He has gone to the market.'

I was about to walk away when she asked, 'Are you leaving, Georgootty?' Her hair had come loose. She gathered it and pulled it into a careless knot, a secretive smile playing on her red lips. She bent her head, slowly.

My heartbeat quickened as I climbed on to the veranda. As she pulled up an old wicker chair, I looked at her plump forearms; her body filled my vision with an ache. I thought she'd stand there chatting with me, but that was not what happened. She went inside the house without another word and, after a while, the window above my head opened a crack. I could see her long fingers, lustreless nails embedded in their fleshy ends.

Scared, I look around.

Suddenly, the sun went behind a cloud and the little tree in the yard became hazy. The shadow coming down the hill enveloped me in a thin yet protective blanket.

I went inside. In the darkness inside the house, an unfamiliar smell welcomed me.

Memories, and the hazy blanket in which they were wrapped, were still within me. Pressing the warm nakedness of her aroused breasts to my chest, she whispered urgently, 'Georgootty, you don't know anything.'

The sun was back with a vengeance when I stepped out into the yard, my head bowed and my feet heavy and tired. I didn't have the courage to look back. I walked as quickly as I could along the narrow path in the undergrowth, arriving, breathless, at the stream sparkling in the sun. I huddled down by its side and splashed water on my face. My tears mingled with the sun-warmed water.

13.

He's crying. He's crying again.

No one sees him, no one hears him. Indeed, no one understands him.

His voice travels down the hill, carried by the tired cold wind blowing through the dark and dew-drenched lanes. Finding no other place to rest, it settles in my ear.

Seven days ago, on a dewy frigid night, I heard his cries. His cries might have come searching for me before, but on that night I listened. His cries are a beacon to the last of my sorrows, to endless contentment. I realized that.

He's crying. He's crying again just for my ears. Unabated in his longing, he cries over and over again.

14.

Pappachan used to be my friend. In fact, he used to be my closest companion until the death of Mathan.

Pappachan was Babychayan's driver and, as such, I could

claim some kind of authority over him, but I never wielded it. Despite the age difference between us, I used to joke with him and tell him things, even my secret dreams and desires. That's how much I trusted him.

Pappachan was almost forty years old, but the thought of finding a woman and settling down seemed to have bypassed him. I asked him about this one day and he said, 'My dear Georgootty, do you take me for a fool? Why should I get married when other people have wives?' He then looked at me and laughed, long and low.

I am not sure when I got friendly with him and became a willing audience to his stories of conquest.

'You know Thresya, Kurian's missus? She's fully into me. Oh, Georgootty, that woman's got style.'

Pappachan's stories were entertaining. They surprised me, made me question my beliefs. And yet, sometimes, without any particular reason, they also frightened me.

I've tried to make myself hate him. But then I think: Why should I hate him? He's not doing anything wrong. In this world, men and women are attracted to each other and yearn to be with each other. This one-man-one-woman rule is just for convenience. The truth is that everyone is looking for as much happiness and variety as possible when it comes to sexual relationships.

Pappachan did not force himself on any woman. He only slept with women who, clandestinely, invited him to their beds. Perhaps he seduced them, cast a net for them, but these women were perfectly capable of avoiding unwanted attention and protecting themselves from potentially dangerous liaisons. It's not Pappachan's fault that they were attracted to him. He was

a handsome man, with a golden body, tireless eyes and voluptuous lips. He was a lucky man.

'Women! Oh, they are something else! Do you know why
God put them on this earth?' he would ask, and then proceed
to answer his own question. I didn't spend much time analysing his answers, nor did I think of them later. I got something
from Pappachan that I didn't find anywhere else. His stories
aroused me.

The first time I felt a seed of hatred for Pappachan sprout
in my mind was when he talked about Cecily. Even then, I
squashed it and continued to keep his company.

'Georgootty, you're a lucky man.'

'Why do you say that?'

'That Cecily—she is in love with you.'

'How do you know that?' I asked, shocked.

'You don't worry about how I know. But it's true. She is in
love with you.'

He didn't wait for me to answer before continuing, 'She's
trouble, but I knew that. She borrowed some money from me
and I knew I wasn't going to get it back. So what? I got what I
wanted. Yesterday afternoon, her mother and father were not at
home. Praise be to Christ! So I went, and when it was all over,
she said she wanted to see you, wondered why you don't go
there any more.'

I didn't sleep that night, and the next day, I tried to avoid
him. But when I saw him the day after that, I couldn't help
but smile at him. He hadn't done anything wrong, I said to
myself. Cecily could have repaid that loan if she wanted to,
but she didn't try. She was not the type to worry about these
things.

I rationalized each of Pappachan's conquests, shared in his victory and happiness. That was until Mathan's death.

Mathan died while running contraband rice from Kodagu. When he went off with his friends, taking the forest lanes, Pappachan and I were hanging out at the cemetery. Pappachan said, 'Poor sod! He's off, trampling through the forest to make a dime or two. Praise Jesus! I've been after his wife since last Christmas and, finally, this morning she said yes. All I have to do now is to go there tonight. She'll be waiting for me with tapioca and fish curry. No need to worry about anyone or anything until midnight.'

Pappachan left me and walked down the hill. At the bottom, where the lane forked away near the njeral tree, he stopped, turned toward me and waved.

Mathan died that night.

They were on their way to the rice farmer's house, their cloth-covered torches lighting only where they put their feet, walking stealthily through the forest, scared of informants. They were on unfamiliar terrain in the pitch dark. They never got to the farmer's house, the wretched path forsook them. Mathan, who was leading the way, fell into a disused well and, stuck in the mud and weeds, he drowned.

Next day, at dusk, Mathan's dead body was brought home from the forest, hoisted on the shoulders of his mates. Pappachan was among those who gathered to watch at the wayside. On that day, he became my enemy. I never spoke to him again, never even smiled at him.

Tomorrow, when they sit me down in the back of the jeep and drive me away, Pappachan will experience the pleasurable feeling of vengeance. There will be a new light in his eyes.

15.

I was on my own when I met Lucy. Pappachan parked the jeep by the front gate of Cholakkal Estate and started walking in with me, paying no attention when I told him that I wanted to go in alone. I had to be stern with him before he decided to wait at the gate.

The lane from the estate gate to the bungalow was shady and cool, the abundant greenery of coffee bushes all around. I imagined walking down that lane, hand in hand with Lucy. The thought embarrassed me and I quickly shook it off like a drop of unexpected dew. Still, a sense of happiness lingered in my mind like a drizzle in sunshine.

My footsteps quickened as a sense of urgency swelled inside me.

Ouseppachan spotted me from afar and hurried toward me. Shaking my hand, he asked me why I hadn't brought Babychayan along. Like a proper adult, I answered all his questions about the well-being of Anniechechi and her father. There was no anxiety or doubt in my mind. In fact, I was enjoying the way in which Ouseppachan hung on to my words, nodding like an idiot. A certainty that I would be perfectly able to deal with life's ordinary moments gave my words gravitas and my movements control and grace.

Ouseppachan invited me to sit on one of the wicker chairs in the front room. Several men and women came, asking pretty much the same inane questions Ouseppachan had asked me. Everyone knew who I was. Still, they introduced me to each other: 'This is Baby's younger brother.'

Beaming at each other, they continued chattering among themselves, asking and answering their own questions, as if for my sake. Just as their enthusiasm and curiosity began to fade, a short, dark man came out bearing two glasses of orange juice—for me and Ouseppachan. Presently, the people vanished, one by one, into the house, leaving Ouseppachan and me alone in the front room.

Ouseppachan was restless. He commented on the heat outside, comforted himself with the fact that the room itself was cool, drummed on the coffee table with his fingers, then, as if suddenly remembering something, called out, 'Lucy . . .' No one replied. He got up and called again, a bit louder this time.

'Coming,' a reply came from inside the house. Ouseppachan turned to me as if to say something, but changed his mind and looked away.

A tremor ran through me and the courage I had built up drained away. I looked down, concentrating on the faded carpet on the floor. A streak of sweat made its way down my chest.

I sat like that until I heard Ouseppachan clear his throat to get my attention.

The door curtain had been pushed slightly to the side, and a fair, glowing face had been displayed there for me to see. A face as innocent as a child's. I looked at it as though it were a sacred vision. There was a smile on that face, a sliver of sunshine, but it vanished as the expectant eyes, seeking something extraordinary, fell on me. As I waited for the imminent destruction of my being, the face disappeared behind the curtain as if pulled away, and a sound, halfway between a scream and a moan, fell in my ears.

His face drained of colour, Ouseppachan sat there, silent in his unease. Then, we got up together.

'Georgootty, you shouldn't misunderstand,' he said, as we

walked to the gate. 'She is an innocent soul, easily scared when she meets new people.' He took my hand in his and looked, pleadingly, into my eyes.

'You two are yet to get to know each other. This anxiety and fear ... It won't last long. You know how girls ...'

He let out a difficult laugh, leaving his sentence incomplete.

16.

The four of us were sitting on the bare ground in the church-yard—me, Pappachan, Babychayan and Kunnan Jose, a friend of Babychayan who was a party worker.

Months have passed, but I remember it clearly. It was an old dilapidated church. The elderly priest paced the yard, reading from a Bible in a language unfamiliar to us. We sat there for a long time, sucking on a fat ganja beedi, the smoke from which hung over us like mist.

When the Bible reading started to feel like a cry from afar, I got up, followed by Babychayan and Pappachan. Kunnan Jose was the last to get up.

We walked aimlessly, not thinking about where we were going. We couldn't have walked far when, suddenly, by the side of a cluster of rocks, we saw a woman. She was smiling broadly and was completely naked. Pappachan and Babychayan ran toward her. Babychayan pushed Pappachan aside and, right in front of our eyes, he fell upon her like a bull in heat.

The three of us walked on, Kunnan Jose leading the way like a guide. Climbing up a barren hill, we reached a vast meadow. Further ahead, we saw another woman, dark and plump and as naked as the other one, walking toward us. Ignoring me and

Kunnan Jose, Pappachan held out his hand and they fell on to the grassy floor, fumbling with each other.

We carried on, Kunnan Jose and I, presently reaching a rubber plantation. As we walked into the plantation, Kunnan Jose was overcome with a sudden burst of energy. Holding a green branch aloft, he ran around, shouting and screaming. Beyond the tidy rows of rubber trees, there was a country lane covered in dry grass. It had a deserted look, as though no one had walked through it in recent times.

Kunnan Jose touched my shoulder and pointed into the distance. There, in the valley of a dry, barren hill, stood a huge, wild tree—and hanging upside down from one of its branches was a human shape. The strange sight did not bewilder me until, all of a sudden, I realized that the man had been hung from the tree with his feet tied together, and that it was the lifeless body of Appayi.

As Kunnan Jose started laughing at me, I walked up and squatted under Appayi's hanging head. His face was bone-dry, as though drained of all blood and bodily fluids, his eyes invisible underneath lids that were fused firmly into the sockets. Kunnan Jose's loud laughter came roaring like the wind and, in it, Appayi's dead body swung, and its mouth opened as if to say something to me.

Screaming, I opened my eyes.

17.

I wouldn't have met Lucy if Babychayan hadn't stood for elections. And he wouldn't have forced me to go meet her if the Cholakkal family was not as well-off as they were.

The day Babychayan's name was published in the list of

election candidates was the same day I got my exam results. I was on the way back from the college and was walking home from the bus stop, when someone called me from behind, 'Georgootty . . .' It was Pailychettan, on his way back from selling his banana harvest at the cooperative produce society.

He was in unusual form and reeked of mankurni—the local hooch. 'Georgootty, did you hear? Babychayan is a candidate,' he told me. 'It's been announced in today's newspaper. You're a lucky boy. If he wins, he won't be an ordinary MLA. Minister, that's what he'll be. Minister!'

Puffing up his chest and stretching his neck, Pailychettan proclaimed it with a great sense of pride. He must have been disheartened to see the lack of enthusiasm on my face, so he stopped talking. Our heads bent, eyes fixed on the red earth under our feet, we walked on, but I knew he couldn't keep the silence for too long.

'Have you heard who the other party's candidate is?' He looked expectantly at me. I shook my head. 'It's him, that Philip—the one who came holding the flag when Kallan Johnnie was killed. That same fellow.' Pailychettan ground his teeth and spat, 'Thoo . . .' He continued, 'Johnnie was out of order and Babychayan scolded him. So he came at him with a knife. People got involved and he got killed. Why should Philip and the rest of them get all bothered about it? Don't we have the police and courts here to take care of such things?' Pailychettan warmed to his subject, 'Is it he who's feeding Kallan Johnnie's missus? If it wasn't for Babychayan, she and her offspring would have died of starvation by now.'

Pailychettan talked nonstop until he turned into the lane before my house, counting out the flaws of Philip and his friends one by one. And before walking away, he stood close to me and whispered in my ear, 'You must be vigilant, boy. They'll do whatever it takes to win. There's already a rumour going around that you brothers are not all that close.'

There was a jeep with the party's flag and a small crowd in the yard. Babychayan stood, arms folded, in the middle of the crowd, and Kunnan Jose was explaining something important to him. He looked sideways at me before turning his attention back to Kunnan Jose.

I went straight to my room, shut the door and fell on my bed. I reminded myself that I had failed my exams, but it didn't generate any particular sadness in me. My mind was still like a fallen leaf, unable to absorb anything new.

The walk in the hot sun had given me a headache. I got up, took off my shirt and hung it on the clothesline, switched on the fan and lay back on the bed. The rivulets of sweat on my body dried in the cool air of the fan, and I lay peacefully focusing on that coolness. Like a breeze descending the hill, sleep settled on my eyelids.

I woke up hearing Babychayan's footsteps. He pulled up a chair and sat next to the bed.

'Georgootty, you failed your exams, didn't you?' he asked. 'Ah, well, it's not that big a deal. The Punnakkunnel dynasty is not going to end because of it.' His voice was slack and imbued with the dry smell of moonshine.

'Don't you worry, Georgootty,' he continued. 'I am a candidate, and if I win, I will be a minister. You know, giving me this seat is a calculated move. Last time, Joseph won by just two thousand votes. He's an outsider and, what's more, he has not returned to this constituency even once after he won. Kunnan

Jose pointed this out to him and he withdrew. And if I don't step up, the others will take this seat. You know Philip—he is cunning and he is local.'

He looked me straight in the eye and said in a low voice, 'We can guarantee my win, but I need your help.'

'My help?' I asked.

Babychayan laughed. 'You know the Cholakkal folk. They are a big family, and between their daughters and in-laws and relatives and old people, they have over two thousand votes in this constituency—and we won't lose a single one of them if you take an interest.'

'You know Cholakkal Ouseppachan,' he went on. 'He has three daughters. Two of them are married. Those two have college degrees. But the third one, Lucy . . . She hasn't been to college, but so what? She's as smart as they come.'

Without giving me a chance to respond, he continued, 'You must do me a favour, Georgootty. I gave my word to Ouseppachan. Go and see that girl. We can take care of the rest later. All we want now is to make them believe that we're serious about this relationship. Let Pappachan know when you're free. And take a couple of friends with you. You know I can't make the time with this election looming. I have a million responsibilities. I am off to Kottayam first thing in the morning with Kunnan Jose.'

Now he was in a hurry. 'Okay, so I can trust you to get this done, can't I? Just go and see her, we can take care of the formalities later. I've talked to Ouseppachan already. Go there, see the girl, have a cup of coffee, a few minutes chitchat and come back. All right?'

18.

Babychayan lost the election.

After the results were announced, he didn't leave the house for a couple of weeks. In the daytime, many people came to see him and pass the time analysing the results and blaming others. He would get rid of them somehow and sit brooding, until Kunnan Jose and his gang arrived in the evening, after which he would buck up. Then they would sit drinking and playing cards late into the night.

One day, early in the morning, Cholakkal Ouseppachan arrived. He had a gang of people with him. I was sitting in the front of the house, reading the newspaper. Babychayan was in the orchard, talking to the workers.

'Is Baby home?' Ouseppachan was in a serious mood. I nodded and was about to go and get him when he appeared.

'I saw you come in. What's up so early in the morning?' Babychayan played it cool. Ouseppachan did not respond, but made a grunting noise.

'You're such a big shot, aren't you?' One of the men in Ouseppachan's gang said. 'We reckoned we might not get to see you if we didn't come so early.'

Before he could finish, Ouseppachan intervened, 'I guess I have to explain to you why we are here.'

'You think you can trick us?' asked a short young man. 'You can pull out of the marriage proposal by spreading rumours about Ouseppachan's daughter being pregnant. But don't think you can swindle us out of the money you borrowed.'

Babychayan stood there with his head bowed, silent.

'Where's our money?' The short man shouted and grabbed

Babychayan by the collar. A scuffle ensued and, hearing the commotion, the workers in the orchard came running.

Ouseppachan gave him an ultimatum, 'I'll give you until tomorrow morning. Bring the money to my bungalow.' He then turned to me and said, 'Come down here if you have the guts. Your brother took two lakhs rupees from me, saying that you'll marry my daughter.'

They left chattering among themselves. I didn't pay attention. As if from a long way off, I heard the insipid sound of Anniechechi's insincere tears.

19.

Finally I escaped. Or so I thought.

I reached a vast, tree-lined clearing. I lay down there, still and straight in the moonlight, with the lush greenery all around me. I was not afraid, not anxious, and my heart beat steadily in my chest. The tremor I had been feeling for the past several days vanished.

I'd left home in the stillness between the fading evening light and the moonrise, making sure Babychayan and Anniechechi did not see me leave. The screen of mist below the darkening sky provided me strength and protection along the country lanes.

For the next six or seven days, as Babychayan and his people searched for me, I lived in the forest. As they wandered in the forest looking for me, I sat on a precipice marvelling at the bottomless chasm below, provided company to a rock plantain standing lonely in the indifferent silence at the top of the forest, lost myself among the wild arrowroot and in the quiet pleasure of springs flowing down the rocks.

In the cold nights, magnificent old trees kept me company, as I sat among their branches pressing my body against their rough barks; they kept me warm even as I was soaked in the night dew. I listened to the sacred song of the sap coursing eternal through their veins. Slowly, the echo of the forest and the thousand strange noises eased away. Night became a lake. A peaceful lake asleep amidst the shade of bamboo clumps.

And in the morning, when the first light of a new day touched me, I swayed like a blade of grass, laughed out loud at a porcupine running noisily away, startled out of his hideout. I spent the day following the monkeys jumping from branch to branch, tracking the footprints of wild fowl through the undergrowth.

I gorged on ripe jackfruit and chewed tamarind leaves to get rid of their intense sweetness. Wild cherries, thechi fruit, koovalam—there was plenty to eat in between, as I walked for miles up steep rises, slopes and unexpected bends of forest lanes. There was no anxiety, no thoughts about the future, as my days passed within the seemingly eternal protection of the forest.

One afternoon, I swam like a minnow in the river warmed gently by creeping shards of sunlight. After my swim, I lay sunning myself, stark naked, on the rocks rising out of the water. I could smell the fragrance of some unknown flower in the breeze. The whisper of the leaves and the endless chirruping of the cicadas filled my ears. The weary murmur of a nearby stand of bamboo was almost dreamlike, as I slipped slowly into a slumber, sedated by the warm smell of the rocks as they baked in the sun.

I did not hear a noise or have an inkling of danger, yet I

woke up abruptly and, with a sense of alarm, I opened my eyes. I saw Appayi clutching on the rocks, with his arm extended toward me. Babychayan and Pailychettan stood on the bank of the river and, next to them, Pappachan stared at me with a piece of dry wood in his hand.

I did not scream or try to run in a pointless attempt at escaping. When Appayi took my hand, I got up obediently and followed him across the now muddied water to where Babychayan stood waiting. I felt Pailychettan's rough hand on my waist, as he tied the towel he had on his shoulder around me. And then, as if following an already laid plan, we fell into step behind Babychayan, who led us away and out of the forest.

20.

I am Georgekutty, son of Punnakkunnel Varki. I am twenty-two years old, although you might think I am older. I am taller than average, but that too might be an illusion as I am very thin. I look exhausted and dispirited, like a person with some disease of the liver. My protruding cheekbones give me the look of a poor person, but, if you pay attention to my walk and bearing, you will see that I am from a well-to-do family.

Like most people, I too am happenstance. My wishes or permission were immaterial to my being born, the basic structure and shape of my mind and body predestined. The changes I could make to them were miniscule. Then there are the circumstances in which I lived and grew up. These were also pre-selected and prepared, their strength and cruelty unspeakable.

Tomorrow morning, they will wake me up and take me to the city. I am not sure what will happen after that. I cannot even guess when I will be back. Perhaps, tonight, Georgekutty will cease to exist. Instead, there will be another person with the same name. I can imagine how he would look and the state of his mind: shaven head, puffy cheeks, overweight body, eyes shrouded by a constant mist of cheerlessness. He will sit peacefully in a corner, unable to see or hear anything real. Everyone will find his gloomy smile tiresome, and his uneasy presence will cloak the house like a sickness.

21.

It is through touch that I know myself. I stroke my own cheeks in an uncontrollable sense of longing. The softness of my hands presses against my throat, wanders across my hairless chest, sunken stomach, travels further down to my tired genitals. My fingers tremble as they discard them and reach for my emaciated thighs, my twig-like legs, and my feet with their visibly swollen veins.

I am Georgekutty. A long road to nowhere. A pointless pasture, green only on the inside. An endless repetition, like a bundle of used clothes.

When I ran away from home and lived in the forest for six or seven days, I wasn't seeking new experiences or looking for some rare raw materials to build a new life. I was not even seeking an adventure. I went, like a migratory bird, following my basic instincts, looking only for food and water, warmth and coldness which made life possible. Perhaps it is incorrect to compare myself to a migratory bird, an attempt, through imagining wings, to elevate myself from my otherwise impoverished life. I must have known—desired even—that, before long, I would be caught and brought back to be treated differently, to be protected and, thus, freed from even the mundane expectations of ordinary life.

Georgekutty knew that he had no part in the injustices of this world, and yet he tried to interpret them, rationalized them even when they crushed him in their strong embrace. He found himself to be at fault, wallowed in the loneliness of this guilt, suffering, with a strange sense of responsibility, the meaningless thoughts that rose like bubbles.

His world was one devoid of velocity. He stood rooted in one place for years, not desiring to experience anything. All that happened in his life passed him by, touching him but not giving him the experience of being touched, like a breeze that passed through leaves without moving them or making them whisper.

Every day, he took stock, adding and subtracting, accurately calculating each of his faults. He believed, with great arrogance, that he knew how to correct them. He was careful and meticulous in his analysis of himself. The thoroughness of his self-criticism was a source of great pleasure for him, something that his soul celebrated.

Stillness coalesced above him like an ancient rock formation, and he, an insect, frolicked underneath its dark and dank pathways. It was not for freedom that his body and mind yearned, nor for the pleasures of those meanderings. He could, in fact, have shrugged off its hold if he wanted. Instead, he stayed, tasted the same fruits and leaves over and over again, relived the same fears that had once gnawed at his heart, endlessly pacing its passages.

22.

I am Georgekutty, Punnakkunnel Varki's son George. I am superfluous, unwanted, an ugliness marring the surface of the earth.

I can't get enough of myself. I can't get enough of touching, feeling, knowing myself. I cannot bring myself to share my being.

I am an ancient turtle, eating and excreting the solitude under a gentle blanket of weeds in a dew-fed pond in the forest. I do not like sunlight or the warmth of the day. The footsteps that echo along the edge of the pond scare me.

I am hunger and nourishment. I cannot desire for anything more.

Inside the armour of silence, my words rise and fall repeatedly, strike a rhythm audible only to my ears. Like a lullaby, it enfolds me, and I doze only to wake up yearning to hear it again.

And now, finally, I am satiated. These repetitions, distasteful to you like the dance of threadworms, are coming to an end. I will do you a favour.

23.

He is crying. He is crying again.

No one sees him, no one hears him. No one, perhaps, even knows about him. Blinded by his yearning, he keeps on crying. His voice, unable to find purchase elsewhere, falls trembling into my ears, spreads like daylight over my eyes.

There is not much left of this night, and before it is gone, I will show him mercy. I will satisfy his desires. I will give him true love.

24.

The gun is still here. It is unlicensed and it belonged to Appachan. In its memory are the burning eyes of tigers, the ripped-up hood of a cobra, the countless cries that have shocked the forest.

I have known of it since my childhood, watched it fearfully from a safe distance. Today, for the first time in my life, I take it in my hand.

When he set out into the forest to search for me, Babychayan had brought this secret weapon with him. He had it with him when I walked into this room holding on to Appayi's hand. He forgot to take it with him when he left after locking me up in this little room in the middle of the four bedrooms on the top floor. Perhaps he was exhausted after several days of wandering through the forest.

The gun usually sits in the space between the safe and the wall in Babychayan's room. It is good that it has been misplaced for the first time. If not, how would I answer his cries? Protect his faith in me? What other secret weapon could I use to lead him toward eternal salvation?

Just before dawn, Pappachan woke up. He scrambled out of his bed, hearing the death cry of a wild goat. He looked around the yard and shone his torch among the trees. He was sure that the sound was quite close by. Even if the wounded animal had run away, there would be the sound of the hunters running after it, their whispers, but there was nothing. Everything remained quiet.

When he returned, disappointed, Baby and his wife were in the veranda. They too had been woken up by the death cry and had come outside to see what was going on.

As if to explain something, all three of them opened their mouths at the same time but stopped and stood looking at each other with their mouths still open. Then, persuaded by something uncanny, they walked inside and toward the staircase, as if in a trance. As they climbed the stairs, their feet treading softly on the steps, they heard the last grunts of a dying wild goat. Their nostrils filled with the hot smell of its ebbing life blood.

Kaattadu, 1987

tender coconut

1.

For the last twenty years, I have been a consulting psychologist at Dr Murukan's clinic. In the beginning, it was just the two of us. I would never know how, almost two decades ago, he'd had the courage to open a psychiatric clinic in this hillside village. In those days, people did not look for psychiatric treatment in cases of madness. There would be times when a mad person was aggressive, and then he or she would be forcibly taken to the well-known psychiatric hospital in the city. Usually, however, mad people remained in the community, causing mild discomfort to themselves and others. The elders tolerated them—'poor thing is not right in the head,' they'd say—while the youngsters looked for ways to have a bit of fun with them.

Dr Murukan opened his clinic in a two-storey building—two rooms on each floor, and a largish lean-to and a bathroom downstairs. He had bought the building from Chanthan Mooppan, who had an amputated arm and who is now dead. Mooppan had it built when he was flush with money from lease-farming black pepper and ginger and selling coconuts in Coorg. People used to call it 'Stumpy's mansion'. When I was young, I'd heard two different stories about how Chanthan Mooppan lost his left forearm. In one story, he'd lost it in a bus accident somewhere between Virajpetta and Moornadu, while in the other an altercation with a Kodava was the cause. I can still picture him, hurrying down the road to inspect his newly constructed building, the amputated end of his arm wrapped up in a cotton towel. Every day, at 9 AM sharp, just as I'd be waiting for my school bus. That was the only time he came to the market area, as far as I could tell.

In those days, there was barely anything to be called a market there—just a mud road for bullock carts, a shop that sold buttermilk to passers-by, and a kanji shop. People must have wondered whether Mooppan was right in his head to build a mansion in this back of beyond corner of the hills. By the time Mooppan passed on and Dr Murukan bought the building from his son Unnikkannan, times had changed and, along with it, our corner of the world. The mud road was tarmacked. A two-storey building replaced the buttermilk shop, with a coolbar below and Sujith Jyotsar's astrology shop above. The thatched hut that was the kanji shop made way for Hotel Ruchi, and next to it there was a brand new bus shelter with the sign, 'Kelanchira Stop'.

Where there once was barely any footfall, there was now substantial activity until late into the night—people waiting for the bus, a cacophony of vehicles, young people whiling away their time. Even then, when Dr Murukan hung the sign for the new clinic in front of Chanthan Mooppan's building, people said, 'A mad doctor to treat the mad! Would anyone in their right mind start such an enterprise here?'

I hadn't shared that opinion, even at the beginning. There was a reason for it. I'd done an MA in psychology, a PG diploma in guidance and counselling and an MPhil in consulting psychology, and was beginning to think about starting my own practice at home. One morning, a couple of weeks after Dr Murukan opened his clinic, I went to see him. Exuding a self-confidence that I didn't quite feel, I introduced myself to him and asked, 'Could you accommodate me here, Doctor? Just think of it as a temporary arrangement until I gain some experience.' The good doctor didn't raise any objection; instead, he nurtured my fledgling self-confidence: 'Yes. I was looking for someone like you. The patients who come here don't really need any treatment. What they usually need is counselling.'

Dr Murukan's fee in those days was twenty rupees. Admittedly a bit steep for that area, and even though there were some rumblings about it, no one raised any actual objections. The locals regarded Dr Murukan and me as not being of any particular use to them. Dr Murukan told me on the first day, 'Vivek, you must also charge the same fees as me. Don't make any concessions. The patients should not feel that the job you do is in any way inferior to what I do. So, charge twenty rupees for each session.'

I was somewhat reluctant at first, but decided to take the doctor's advice. It helped that most of our patients were not local but came from the small towns and villages further away. Not being acquainted with them or their families reduced my discomfort in charging them twenty rupees per session.

I was assigned one of the downstairs rooms as my consultation room. Dr Murukan worked upstairs. I had strict instructions that only those whose problems could not be solved by counselling and talking therapy and needed further treatment should be sent upstairs. There were barely four or five such cases a day. So, in effect, when I made around two hundred rupees a day, the Doctor only made eighty or hundred rupees. At first, I was concerned that this might create some friction between us. But Dr Murukan didn't seem to mind, and his attitude toward me didn't change. Nevertheless, I devised a plan whereby patients who needed medical attention for physical ailments—those with high blood pressure, and with sodium or hormone imbalances—were sent up to him with little chits describing the problem. In that way, I managed to send at least half of the patients to him. Even then, he didn't react and continued dealing with me as usual. As time went on, I began to feel that there was something secretive about him, something beneath the surface. He was evasive and tended to respond to personal questions with one-word answers. I found myself beginning to speculate about his behaviour, and when my thoughts started getting uncomfortable, I resolved to stop probing into his affairs and to let him come to me if and when he wanted to talk.

Apart from me and the patients, the only other people Dr Murukan talked to were the waiters and the cashier at Hotel Ruchi. He never talked about his personal affairs and shared nothing about his family or his hometown. In the clinic, he seemed energetic and happy, but outside it he wore a dark cloak of severity. Not many people dared to engage in small talk with him.

There is bound to be a moment in everyone's life when one feels the uncontrollable need to open up to a fellow human being. I was certain that, before long, Dr Murukan would also feel this urge. I was not wrong.

2.

One day, when the day's consultations were over and it was time to close, Dr Murukan came to me and said:

'Vivek, if you're not in a hurry, why don't you sit down for a while?'

'Of course, Doctor, I'm not in a hurry.'

The Doctor seemed relieved. We talked late into the night. I say 'we', but the truth was that he talked and I sat there listening to him with great interest.

'Vivek, you don't know anything about me, do you?' he said by way of an introduction. 'Who I am, who my family is, or why I came to this new and unfamiliar place to open a clinic. I feel that you should know all this even if no one else does.'

What followed was a flood of words. He talked about his father, now dead, a younger brother who appropriated all the family wealth, a cunning sister-in-law who turned his mother against him with her manipulations, the sense of utter loneliness and alienation he felt within his family, the confrontation he had with the management of the hospital where he began his career, the narrow escape from two separate goonda attacks, forgetting to get married amidst all the chaos in his life, the slow development of misogyny and a general disinterest within him . . . several such incidents. His descriptions of some of these events seemed strange. The intricate details he went into when narrating some of the earliest events in his life made me marvel at his memory, even as I started wondering about his state of mind. The sights he saw on a boat trip with his father when he was six or seven years old, including a big snake crawling along a deserted and disused jetty—these descriptions were so exquisite that I felt I was witnessing them myself. The description of the time he spent working in a hospital in Chennai where, on most nights, he had dinner with a beautiful Telugu eye special-ist was the most resplendent with details. As he narrated how she got engaged to a cardiologist, all the while pretending to be in a relationship with him, the Doctor was overcome with emo-tion, his voice cracking and his eyes wet.

Whenever he felt that he was being overly emotional, the Doctor brought himself back to normality by reciting a couple of lines from *Thirukkural* or some other ancient Tamil text to support the idea that such incidents were natural and common in human existence. After the first couple of times, I began to find this strategy tedious.

The Doctor concluded his monologue by describing the unbearable mental anguish he felt on the nights he spent alone at the clinic. By the end, I began to suspect that perhaps he was on the brink of being clinically depressed. However, quite sud-denly his demeanour changed and, as if he had experienced some sort of catharsis, he became upbeat and happy.

'Oh, look at the time. We forgot all about dinner. Come, let's go find some food—kanji and chammanthi, or perhaps some tapioca with fish curry. Whatever you fancy.'

'No, sir. I think I'll go home and have dinner. They will be waiting for me at home.'

He didn't insist, but made me walk with him to Hotel Ruchi, where he continued talking for another half hour standing by the roadside. It was only when a lorry pulled up in front of the hotel and the workers charged into the hotel like a starving horde that he finally decided to go in and have his dinner.

The road home was wet with dew, the rubber trees cast dark shadows in the moonlight. As I walked along, I inadvertently spoke aloud: 'The Doctor's case seems to be so much more complex than all the other patients' I have seen so far.'

But that turned out to be an isolated incident. After that night, I never had occasion to be concerned about Dr Murukan's mental state. Nothing in his behaviour or conversation since has made me think that way, and he never again talked to me about his private life.

3.

Much has changed in my life in the twenty years I have worked with Dr Murukan. I have learned a hundred times more about people and the experiences of distress and trauma that they undergo than I had ever learned as a psychology student. And although I never actually trained in psychiatry, I acquired a certain level of understanding about mental illnesses and how to treat them.

I would quite like to write about at least some of the thousands of clients I have seen during this not inconsiderable amount of time. But I am only going to write about one of them, a person with whom, for some unknown reason, I felt a strong connection. Without further delay, let me tell you his story, a story that will also take my readers through some of the important chapters in my own life.

Two or three months into my practice, I spent an entire morning until about lunchtime with a patient named Mohanan, a seller of tender coconuts at a temple named Kudungomkaavu. Despite the time I spent with him, I was left with no useful insight into his problems. I was exhausted and could muster up the energy to see only one more patient. I sent the other ten or so in the waiting room away, saying that I had to go somewhere urgently.

I told the same lie to Dr Murukan, left the clinic, went home and straight to bed. I must have slept for about twenty minutes, and when I woke up, all I could see was the face of that tender coconut vendor, a face as innocent as that of a young child.

He spoke as if he were narrating a simple story, but the experiences and problems that unfolded in his story were complex and many layered. Where is Kudungomkaavu? How does one get there? I asked him these two questions, directly and indirectly, but he evaded answering them. He said his name was Mohanan and that he was from Eranmoola. I recognized the name of the place, but had no real idea where it was. In any case, I was able to guess with some level of certainty that Kudungomkaavu was in Eranmoola.

Kudungomkaavu had a unique attribute, Mohanan said. Instead of a male priest, the pooja there was conducted by seven unmarried women, one on each day of the week. If the priestess of a particular day was menstruating, one of the others did the pooja twice that week. Taking days off and working extra days was an intrinsic part of their role. This rule, that the deity of Kudungomkaavu—Kudungothappan—could not have a male priest and must be attended to by unmarried women priests, and a different one each day, was apparently set right at the time the temple was built.

It was a small temple. Every Friday evening, there was a kettiyaattam, a ritual performance, the expenses for which were usually paid for by one of the devotees as an offering for

Kudungothappan's blessing. There were many who believed that Kudungothappan's blessing would fulfil dreams of a good marriage, fertility, foreign travel and so on.

Throngs of worshippers would begin arriving at the kaavu right from the morning on Fridays, their numbers reaching at least two hundred by evening. On other days too, the temple was popular, averaging a hundred devotees a day. Mohanan sold tender coconuts at the kaavu premises for seven or eight months in a year, the sales peaking in the months of March, April and May, and ending as the rains arrived by the end of May.

Mohanan's merchandise came from the coconut palms growing in the ten-cent plot around his house and from his neighbours' lands. He would climb the trees early in the morning, harvest enough coconuts to sell over the next couple of days, and climb them again on the third day. He would pack them into four gunny sacks, which he carried on his shoulder to the makeshift stall in front of the temple—a palm-leaf thatch on four bamboo posts. A boy from the neighbourhood, Sreelal, accompanied him and the first sack of coconuts, and waited there until Mohanan transferred all four sacks into the stall. It would be a quarter past nine by then, and time for Sreelal to go to school.

He made barely enough money to make ends meet. The rainy season brought more misery, and he had to make do with whatever odd-jobs he could find. He regretted having dropped out of school—if he hadn't, he could have at least found work as a peon and not had to struggle quite so much. He said that he found it difficult to fall asleep on some nights; he twisted and turned in his bed, mired in his worries, and got up exhausted in the morning with no energy to go to work.

Months would pass by tediously until the hot and sultry days were back again.

'You know, Doctor, at first no one paid much attention to my little business,' Mohanan told me. 'But slowly the kaavu management people seemed to realize that I was making a living there and began grumbling. They pestered me about clearing away all the husks and debris every evening, demanded a rent of twenty rupees per day for the use of the premises, and insisted that I leave before the Friday evening rush started . . . I thought that was it—moths in my gruel, end of my livelihood. Then this amazing thing happened. One afternoon, the Thursday priestess, a woman named Chithra, came up to my stall and bought a coconut. I refused to take her money even though she was quite insistent. "No, no, you don't need to pay me for this," I kept saying. So then she tricked me. "Okay then, I won't ever drink another one of your tender coconuts," she said, all serious. I had to give in then and take her money. In fact, she paid me a rupee more than the usual price and wouldn't take it back from me.

'She came again the next Thursday, all friendly like, asking me my name and whereabouts. "Why do you always stand out here? You could come into the temple at least on the days I am here, no?" I felt I should say something to her but couldn't think of anything, so I asked her name. "I know you know my name already, but I'll tell you anyway. It is Chithra," she said and gave me this weird smile.

'For the next four or five Thursdays, without fail at noon, Chithra came for her tender coconut. It began to feel as if the only reason I was going to the kaavu with my coconuts was to see her. But then, just like that, she stopped coming. Another priestess took over her day. I was heartbroken. But since I didn't have another option, I continued going there and selling my coconuts from morning to late afternoon, until the sun was low in the sky.

'Not long after, like moonlight in the darkness of my life, one of the other priestesses came to my stall and bought a coconut. Madhuri, the Monday priestess. Mustering up my courage, I asked her, "Do you know what happened to Chithra, the priestess who used to come on Thursdays? Haven't seen her in a while. Is she okay? Not ill or anything?"

'Madhuri frowned and gave me a withering look. "She was fired because of bad behaviour. I hope you are satisfied."

'The rough edge to her voice made it sound as though it was somehow my fault that Chithra had lost her job. She seemed very angry at me as she stomped back into the temple.

'That evening, one of the kaavu managers came to my stall and demanded a coconut as though he were entitled to it. He drank the water and tossed the shell away. "Mohanan," he said, "you are selling coconuts here purely because of our generosity. Otherwise, you'd be gone from here in a matter of minutes. Don't you dare forget it. You are not qualified to pass comments on who we hire or fire here."

'My throat went completely dry. I couldn't speak. In any case, what would have been the point in answering back? I just stood there trembling.

'I went home deciding that I'd not go back there. But when morning came, I couldn't just stay at home, so off I went to the kaavu as usual, carrying my coconuts. The sales were just beginning to pick up when a political-party leader near my house, Chandrettan, and a few other people came to the stall.

'There was not even a shadow of friendliness on Chandrettan's face. "Our district meeting is coming up," he said in a gruff voice. "You must make a donation of hundred rupees."

'I was shocked. "What are you saying, Chandretta? How can I afford hundred rupees?"

'I don't think he liked me addressing him with the familiar "Chandretta". His face darkened. "There's no need to waste time arguing over it. Give him a receipt for fifty rupees," he said to one of his gang.

'Handing over money I could barely afford was hard. But my troubles didn't end there as I found out the next morning. Someone had trashed my stall—the bamboo poles were pulled up and lay broken in half. There were a couple of people there taking photographs, people I didn't recognize, dressed in dull green khaddar kurtas and grey trousers. "We didn't destroy your shop," one of them told me. "We heard that this shop was responsible for making the temple surroundings dirty and came to investigate. It was already trashed when we got here. So what will you do now? Will you continue your business here?"

'I didn't reply. They said if I continued selling coconuts there, I'd have to make sure that the husks were cleared away and the surroundings kept clean. They mentioned the name of some organization and said that it was their job to ensure that our town was clean and environmentally friendly. I kept my mouth shut. And that was it—my little business selling tender coconuts at the temple was done. Now I try to get by doing whatever odd jobs I can get. It's okay when there's regular work. But there is a new problem around here. People expect you to spend at least a third of your daily wages on foreign liquor. If you're not ready to do that, you can forget about having any kind of human companionship.

'That's my life now—lonely, no friends, no company. And I can't stop thinking about Chithra. I'm not brave enough to go looking for her, to find out where she lives and all that. It would be good to have someone to talk to about all this, but I have no one. I haven't been able to sleep properly either—I just lie there at night, with all these thoughts rushing through my mind. That's really why I came, Doctor, to see whether you could give me some medicine that will let me sleep.'

Mohanan narrated this entire story almost in one breath. By the time he finished, he was panting. His face was pale and he repeatedly tried to lick his dry lips. 'Here, drink some water,' I said, offering him a bottle of water.

A couple of mouthfuls seemed to revive him a little. He sat forward, eager to hear what I had to say.

'You don't have any habits like smoking or drinking, do you?'

'No. I used to smoke beedis, but gave up a couple of years ago.'

'Well, that's good. Have you ever had a fall? I don't mean a little fall on a slippery floor or anything like that. Something more serious, say from a height, where you may have hit your head?'

'No.'

'Have you felt you can't retain things in your memory for long?'

'No, Doctor. I have no such difficulties.'

'Are you in the habit of reading books?'

'No.'

'Never read a book?'

'Only school books.'

'And how far did you get in school?'

'Until class seven.'

'Why did you drop out?'

'We couldn't afford it any more. My father passed away and my mother, well, she's always been sickly. If I didn't go to work, nobody would've eaten.'

'What sort of work did you find then?'

'In a grocery store, as a helper.'

Pretending to remember something suddenly, I pulled open my desk drawer and took out three postcard-sized pictures. They were all of women. One showed a young woman in her late teens wearing a salwar kameez, the other a middle-aged woman in a silk sari. The third was a picture, taken from the back, of a rural woman carrying a pot of water on her hips, and clad in a white mundu and blouse that showed off her shapely behind— a picture that was sure to attract the attention of any man.

I passed them over to Mohanan. 'Tell me,' I said. 'Which of these pictures do you like most?'

Mohanan did not take very long to decide and, as I'd expected, chose the picture of the rural woman.

'Now tell me, does this picture have any similarity with any woman you know? Does it remind you of anyone?'

Mohanan flushed and looked down, as if he couldn't meet my eyes.

'It does, doesn't it? It reminds you of Chithra,' I said without hesitation.

He was overcome with shyness and his hands started shaking.

To help him out of that state, I said, 'Let me ask you something else. Apart from selling tender coconuts and doing odd-jobs, do you have an interest in anything else?'

He didn't seem to understand my question. 'What I mean is, something like a hobby,' I said by way of explanation. 'An interest, perhaps in some sort of craft or music, drawing, sculpture, acting, something like that.'

Mohanan perked up. 'Yes, Doctor,' he said. 'I'm very interested in wood carving.'

'Well, then,' I said, sounding enthusiastic. 'You have nothing to worry about. Anyone good at such a craft can make a good living out of it. If you're willing to put in the effort, you could even become an accomplished artist. I feel you haven't thought about this seriously so far. Here's my suggestion. Why don't you take a month or two and make a couple of wood carvings? Come and see me when you've done that. I'll take care of the rest.'

Mohanan was reluctant. 'Will I be able to sell anything I make, Doctor?'

'We'll see about that. If you can't sell them, I'll buy them myself. Give it a try.'

I gave him three strips of vitamin B12 tablets that a medical representative had left with Dr Murukan. 'Here, take this medicine, one tablet a day after breakfast. Come and see me after one month.'

'Ayyo, Doctor,' Mohanan seemed embarrassed. 'I don't have any money to pay for this.'

'Oh, don't worry,' I said. 'You don't have to pay me for this.'

A broad smile played on Mohanan's face as he got up, placed a twenty-rupee note reverentially on the table, and bowed to me. As he walked out of the consulting room, he was sure-footed and held his head high.

An indescribable feeling of utter exhaustion enveloped me as soon as he left. I knew, with some certainty, that more than half of what he had told me was lies. But he had done an excellent job of creating a seamless and believable narrative out of them, leaving not even a narrow gap for doubt to fester. A not inconsiderable talent.

Mohanan was an ordinary country man. It is unlikely that he was lying about his personal circumstances. What I found hard to believe was the story about the seven priestesses of Kudungomkaavu. Eranmoola, according to Mohanan, was just an hour's bus ride away. I'd surely have heard about a temple so close by with female priests—not one but seven of them. Someone was bound to have written an article about it in one of the newspapers' weekend supplements.

Still, how could a person, especially someone with limited education and no literary talents like Mohanan, make up such a believable story out of something completely untrue? Mohanan did not drink or suffer from any memory problems or other physical ailments. He looked well, a handsome and energetic young man. Usually, it was people with long-standing alcohol problems or some kind of brain injury causing memory impairment who made up such elaborate imaginary experiences. Mohanan had neither of these problems, so why would he . . . ?

4.

As time went by, the clinic began to gain popularity and our workload increased steadily. Dr Murukan began to obsess about adding a pharmacy and an inpatient unit with four or five beds to the clinic. He talked to me about this almost every day. I was adamant that the second idea had to wait until we found suitable premises somewhere close by.

'But we can start the pharmacy as soon as we find a good pharmacist,' I said, when I saw the worried look on his face. 'I'll make enquiries right away. I don't think we'll have to wait long.'

To my surprise, my words came true within a matter of days. The reason was a young man from Eranmoola—Biju, an MA psychology student in his final semester. He'd come to seek my help with finding a topic for his dissertation.

'This is entirely the wrong approach, Biju,' I told him. 'You've already completed three semesters and have only a month and half left until the end of your course. Your first mistake is that you have left the task of finding a topic for your dissertation for the last minute. Your second—bigger—mistake is that you have asked another person to help you. You've got to find your research topic on your own. Discuss it with your guide. If you need any help with exploring practice related issues, I'll be happy to help you as much as I can.'

We chatted for some more time. 'Would you know someone by the name of Mohanan from Eranmoola?' I asked Biju.

'Which Mohanan?' Biju asked. 'I have a neighbour by that name.'

'Did he have a tender coconut business?'

'Yes.'

'Do you know what he is up to these days?'

'He's given up the tender coconut business. He's mostly at home of late, day and night, no work, nothing. He's always been like that. Does some odd-jobs from time to time, and then goes around visiting doctors with made-up stories. Why?' Biju was curious. 'Did he come here with some story?'

I was evasive. Mohanan was my patient and I was duty-bound to keep his confidence. I asked Biju, 'Will you be at home this Sunday?'

'Yes, Doctor.'

'Can I come to your place? I'd like to visit Kudungomkaavu.'

'Why, Doctor?'

'Oh, just personal interest. I'll contact you on Sunday.'

I noted down his telephone number, the information about the bus and directions to Eranmoola before shaking his hand and sending him on his way.

The next Sunday, I took the bus to Eranmoola and met up with Biju. I decided to visit Kudungomkaavu before trying to find Mohanan. The sight of the kaavu came as an utter shock to me. It was very small and sat on top of a steep rise, the yard around it totally overgrown. There was no sign of regular human activity.

'Is there no daily worship here?' I asked Biju.

'No, Doctor. There's a house down there, at the bottom of the hill. They come up and light a lamp at dusk. That's all there is.'

'How long have they been doing that?'

'As long as I can remember.'

'So there is no festival, theyyam, nothing?'

'No,' said Biju. 'Not any more. There might have been in olden times, I don't know.'

I decided not to ask him about the seven priestesses or the Friday festivals. But I felt I needed to visit the people who lit the lamp at the kaavu. Biju took me there.

The house, built in the traditional architectural style, sat at the bottom of the hill. A long path, flanked by flowering shrubs, led to the front of the house from the gate. The land around the house was lush with coconut palms and banana trees, the atmosphere pleasurable and calming. The house owner recognized Biju, but looked somewhat puzzled by the stranger with him.

'I've come to have a look at Kudungomkaavu,' I said, not wanting to prolong his discomfort. 'Biju said you were responsible for the daily lighting of the lamp there. So I thought I'd visit you too.'

'Are you some kind of researcher?'

'No.'

'He is a doctor,' Biju intervened.

'I am a consultant psychologist at a clinic,' I said. 'But I am not here because of my work. I just have an interest in old temples and buildings, just in visiting them, not for research or anything.'

'We do get some visitors who are researchers interested in folklore. That's why I asked. You must pardon me.'

'Oh, don't worry,' I smiled. He introduced himself as Ramakrishnan, a high-school teacher a year away from retirement.

As we continued talking, he turned to the door and called out, 'Chithra, daughter, please bring some tea for our visitors.'

I cannot describe the powerful jolt of electricity that ran through me when I heard him call out the name Chithra. To hide my consternation, I tried to refuse the offer of tea.

'No, no,' said Ramakrishnan. 'What good am I if I can't even offer a cup of tea to someone visiting us for the first time?'

He continued by way of explanation, 'Only my daughter is at home. Her mother has gone to help her sister who's just had an operation. My son is studying at the engineering college in Kasaragod. He only comes home every two weeks or so.'

'And what does your daughter do?'

'She completed a course in pharmacy from Mysore. Worked in a medical shop for a while. But the shop changed hands and she didn't like the new owner's behaviour, so she left. She's been without a job for almost a year now, and is more worried about it than I am. But what to do, it is so difficult to find a job these days.'

As our conversation began to lag with no particular subject, I asked him what sort of god Kudungothappan was.

'A local deity, that's all one can say. In my childhood, there used to be an annual theyyam festival. There is no real story or legend about him. Some people say he was a great saint. Others say he was someone who lived as he pleased, challenging the king and the customs of his community, and was ostracized for it. They say he came here in his old age and died here.' He laughed loudly. 'That second story must be the true one.'

Just as he finished, his daughter came bearing two cups of tea on a tray, placed it in front of us and quickly went back inside. She was in my vision only for a second. I felt as if I were here for a bride-seeing ceremony, and that I had found the right bride on my very first attempt. I'm not sure if Biju or Ramakrishnan saw the change in my expression, but sitting there on the veranda after that was uncomfortable. I was anxious to leave and brought the conversation to a close. As we said our goodbyes and left, I turned and looked at the door, catching a glimpse of a shadow moving swiftly back behind it.

5.

It was late afternoon by the time Biju and I got to Mohanan's house, almost a kilometre away from Kudungomkaavu. The house was small, the walls made of mud bricks. Time-worn roof tiles rested on mouldering rafters. There was no veranda, the front door opened directly on to steps leading to a weed-filled and garbage-strewn gravel yard as neglected as a dis-used country path. The little plot of land around the house was fenced in with ancient seemakkonna, some of which had grown into trees while others sat petrified in their neglect.

The house sat still with no sign of life, but the door was not locked, just pulled shut. Biju called out the name 'Mohanetta' a couple of times, which roused a figure—a woman—who opened the door asking, 'Who's there?' She walked as if she could barely see, her voice and gait frail, although she didn't look much older than about sixty-five.

'Is Mohanettan here?' Biju asked.

'No, son. He's gone out. I'm not sure when he'll be back.' She seemed to have recognized Biju by his voice. 'Who's that with you?'

'He is a doctor, Naniyedathi. He came to see Kudungomkaavu.'

'You'll only be delayed if you wait for Mohanan.'

'That's right. We'll come back later.'

'Was there anything urgent you wanted with Mohanan?'

'Not really. We thought we'd just look him up.'

'Does this doctor know Mohanan?'

I thought it was best if I replied to that question. 'I've met him once. He'd agreed to do a wood sculpture for me.'

'He doesn't do anything nowadays,' she said. 'He used to make wood carvings and earn a bit of money, but not for a while now.'

'Didn't he have a business selling tender coconuts?'

'He never sold them himself. He used to climb the trees and harvest them for other sellers. Sometimes he went with them. He doesn't do any of that any more either.'

'What does he do all day, then?'

'Sits around here mostly, what else? These past few days, he's been going out to see some Swami. Do you know of this Swami, Biju?'

'I've heard about him,' said Biju. 'I hear he's rented the house from Kekke Moolakke Damodarettan's son and started some type of herbal medicine practice. People say he has cures for all manner of illnesses.'

'Ah, that's him,' said the woman. 'Mohanan is his assistant now. Fifty rupees he gets, on top of food and tea.'

It was clear that there was no point in waiting there for Mohanan. We said our goodbyes and left.

I asked Biju if we could go see this Kekke Moolakke Swami.

'Do you absolutely have to see Mohanettan today?' he asked.

'It's not that I have any particular business with him. Just thought it would be good to meet him since I've come all this way, that's all. If you can spare the time, why don't we check out the Swami's ashram?'

'Sure, I don't mind,' said Biju. 'I don't think it is an ashram though, just a small rented house and a couple of disciples. No prayers or spiritual advice or any such thing. Come to think of it, he does what you do. Counselling. Only, he doesn't use that word. Lots of people are going to see him, mostly women, and of course tongues are wagging about that.'

'Come on. Let's go have a look anyway.'

'What will you say to him? Shouldn't you think of a problem to present to him?'

'Don't you worry about that. Is there anyone without a problem that needs solving?'

We were mostly silent as we walked across a parched field and up a steep hill, and finally, soaked in sweat, we reached the Swami's abode.

Biju was right. It didn't look like an ashram, just a concrete building of moderate size, newly painted in saffron. Several people of all ages—mostly women—sat on plastic chairs on the veranda. Mohanan was standing on the veranda. When he saw me, his face blanched and his body hunched like a culprit about to be caught.

I went up to him. 'How are you, Mohanan? Are you well?' A small smile of friendliness appeared on his face. 'I was wondering whether I might be able to see the Swami within the hour. I just want to make his acquaintance.'

'Of course, Doctor,' said Mohanan. 'I can arrange that. One of these women has been waiting since morning. Just wait until she's done, if you don't mind.'

I sat down to wait. The afternoon's session had not begun yet, and it was a while before a signal that the Swami was ready to receive people came from inside the house. Mohanan sent a woman enveloped in a shiny silk sari inside, her plump thirty-five-year-old body wobbled as she walked. More than half an hour passed before she came out, her face flushed and radiant.

'Your turn, Doctor,' Mohanan said.

Inside, a handsome young man sat on a seat covered with gold-coloured silk. There was nothing swami-like about him, except for his saffron robes.

'Why have you come?' he asked me in an artificially soft voice.

'Oh, no particular reason, Swami.' My reply was off-hand. 'I'm a consultant psychologist at a psychiatric clinic in Kelanchira.'

The Swami raised his voice and called out: 'Ramana . . .' His voice had lost its softness and acquired a tone of authority. A middle-aged man, also dressed in saffron, appeared parting the red curtain behind the Swami's seat. He definitely looked like a crook.

Before I could say anything, the Swami turned to this man and said, 'I think I have something in my eye, Ramana.'

'Ayyo, Swami.' The middle-aged man feigned concern and, raising the Swami's face, blew into his eyes. The Swami commenced rubbing his eyes as if that hadn't worked.

'Still there? Come, let's get your eyes washed with rose water, and then you must rest for a while.' The middle-aged man helped the Swami to his feet.

'I'll come back later,' I said. They pretended not to have heard me. I got up and left. I had quite a good idea what kind of 'something' had gotten into the Swami's eyes.

On my way back to the bus stop, and on the bus back to Kelanchira, I was preoccupied with thoughts of Mohanan and Chithra. All those troubling questions about why Mohanan had told me such a cock-and-bull story about Kudungomkaavu came back. I didn't think it was a coincidence that the name of the priestess in his story was Chithra. Had he seen her when she went with her father to light the lamp at the temple, and felt some desire for her? There couldn't have been anything more than that. There was something not quite right about him, given that he'd cooked up a story with such intricate details. Still, I was reluctant to think of him as being mentally ill. I didn't once think that he was telling me lies the whole time he sat across from me and talked. And now I was finding it difficult to think of a reason why he'd chosen to make a fool of me.

6.

As soon as I returned from Eranmoola, I told Dr Murukan about Chithra and, within three days, she was appointed at the clinic as our pharmacist. That was a happy day for me. Her footsteps seemed to bring a fresh life to the clinic.

Chithra brought her own packed lunch to work. One day, as she was having her lunch, I asked her, 'So, are you an accomplished cook?'

'I learned to cook when I was young.' She seemed a little reserved.

'Kudungothappan alone knows what it tastes like,' I teased her.

'I can guarantee you that it tastes better than what you get from Hotel Ruchi.'

I found her confident reply very attractive. We chatted for a while, getting to know each other. I asked her whether she knew anyone named Mohanan in Eranmoola. The name did not seem to affect her; at least her face didn't betray any changes. She had classmates named Mohanan in class eight and ten in school, she said, but she hadn't seen them since. From the way she talked, I didn't feel that she was hiding anything.

I was not the only person who felt that Chithra's arrival brought a new energy to the clinic. The local people also remarked about it. Over a period of time, the clinic grew in popularity and there was an exponential increase in the number of patients coming to see us. Dr Murukan and I seemed to have acquired some level of fame, and our names became familiar to people. Dr Murukan still had to send those who needed inpatient treatment to other hospitals, but now we began to think that it was time to have our own inpatient facilities. Serendipitously, a building became available on the eastern corner of the market square. It had been under construction for two or three years, but there was little progress after the four outer walls were built and, like the local people, I too had thought it would remain in that state forever. To our surprise, one fine day we watched trucks delivering steel bars and concrete, and the very next day the work on the roof started. Within four days, the roof was done.

One night, Dr Murukan asked, 'Vivek, do you know the owner of that new building? Shall we get in touch with him?'

'I know the man—Raghavettan. He had a bakery business in Bangalore and owns several rubber plantations. I think he is looking to rent it out. We could find out.'

'Do you think it would suit our purposes? We need space for at least four or five patients, each with their own room, and bathrooms and other facilities.'

'I'm not sure there will be enough space for en-suite bathrooms. I think he's only planning to build the ground floor for now. We'll have to make do with one shared bathroom and toilet.'

'Well, that will have to do for now,' said Dr Murukan.

'I'd very much like to be able to care for our patients here, at least for the first three or four days, before sending them off to Kozhikode. I don't feel it is right to send them away without doing anything for them, especially given how poor most of them are.'

The next morning, I set out to see Raghavettan. At first, he was not too keen on his building being turned into a psychiatric clinic, but came around when I told him that we were offering to rent the whole building and would pay three months' rent in advance. I hadn't cleared the advance with Dr Murukan, but was confident that he wouldn't object. Anyway, everything worked out and, within three weeks, the inpatient unit started functioning as an extension of the clinic. Dr Murukan found himself an assistant, Dr Sadashivam, an energetic young man despite the old-fashioned name, with a muscular body which convinced everyone that he'd be quite capable of handling any occasional aggression from patients.

Nineteen years later, I still remember, as if it was only yesterday, Dr Murukan introducing Dr Sadashivam to me. We don't often think about how swiftly time passes. The concerns and urgency of everyday life quickly become remnants of memory or forgetfulness. All that remains is the passing of time.

And I can still recall, with great clarity, many of my patients and their myriad problems. My colleagues and I have helped untold numbers of people regain their mental balance. I've run into many of them at weddings and funerals, and they come up to me to show their love and respect. I find myself overcome with emotion at these chance meetings.

The one person I have never run into is Mohanan. A couple of years after I had visited him, I heard from a person who'd come to see me that the Swami in Eranmoola had been violently assaulted. Apparently, he'd behaved indecently toward a woman who had visited his ashram, and her enraged husband hired some thugs to beat him up. They also set fire to the ashram, partially destroying it. The Swami left Eranmoola, and Mohanan lost his job. The last I heard of him was that he'd started selling tender coconuts near the newly opened Cooperative Hospital. That was many years ago. Sometimes, I wondered what he was up to. Was he spending his days within the fantastic world of his own making, lost in its joys and sorrows? Was his mother still alive? Did he ever think of me? Unbeknownst to her, was Chithra really the heroine of his story? I regretted showing him the picture of the rural beauty carrying a pot of water on her waist and asking him whether it reminded him of Chithra. It was entirely inappropriate.

On some days, these circling thoughts consumed me. I admonished myself to get rid of these useless thoughts. My rational mind cautioned me that this was not normal, but I seemed to lose all control when memories of Mohanan crowded into my consciousness. A couple of times, Chithra asked me who I was thinking about so deeply, but my offhand responses seemed to satisfy her curiosity.

Over the years, I had thought of going to Eranmoola to look him up on several occasions, always putting it off on some pretext or the other. Looking back, it is amazing how I have found it impossible to visit someone who lived just about half an hour's car ride away; I couldn't give myself any plausible reason for it. Perhaps there is something deep-rooted in some corner of my mind, something born out of a feeling of betrayal. Or it could be the name Chithra, the heroine of his unsuccessful yet clever story, a name that scared or diminished me in some way.

I am still working at Dr Murukan's clinic. So is Chithra. Sixteen years ago, our relationship progressed from being co-workers to husband and wife. We had two children, two boys. Our earnings increased substantially. Chithra's parents sold their property, the one near Kudungomkaavu, for sixty lakh rupees and moved in with us. My only sister got married and moved to Australia. My parents passed away in consecutive years. The work at the clinic does not interest me any more; I often find myself bored and fed up. Dr Murukan has started showing the fragility and slowness of age, and Dr Sadashivam has taken over the running and supervision of the clinic and the hospital. Raghavettan built a second floor on the building, so now we have all the facilities to treat ten inpatients at once, and are fully booked most of the time. Dr Sadashivam behaves as if all this was due to his capability and drive, and I am sure Dr Murukan is aware of his attitude but is helpless or uninterested. I too, as I said, am bored. I have helped hundreds of people experiencing mental distress, most of them successfully, but I've also had my share of failures. Looking back, the overwhelming feeling I have is not one of satisfaction but of despair.

I have started thinking about giving up my job at the clinic. It would not affect our financial situation. Chithra's parents have been generous, giving us half the money from the sale of their property, and the interest from it alone is sufficient to live on comfortably. I could also continue my practice from home. In fact, if I restricted myself to five clients a day, I would be able to do my job with much more efficiency and honesty.

I had started thinking about it seriously when, one day, Chithra said to me, 'I was wondering . . . Shall we go on a trip?'

'All of us together?'

'Yes. I think my parents are quite bored sitting at home all the time. Let's plan a short trip to a couple of temples in Karnataka or Tamil Nadu.'

'Well, why not?' My response was not filled with enthusiasm. Chithra seemed to take my disinterest to heart, because she didn't bring it up again for over a week. Then one night, as we were getting ready for bed, she said:

'Have you given up on the idea of the trip? I know you are not excited about travelling with the whole family. But I still think we should give it a go. I feel sorry seeing Achchan pottering around at home with nothing to do. He's been very helpful to us. Don't you think it would be nice to do something for him?'

She was right. The trip would also give me a legitimate reason to be away from the clinic for at least a week—a fact that enticed me.

And so we began our preparations. We looked up information about three famous temples in Karnataka, packed enough clothes and other supplies for five days, and set out on our journey early in the morning on a fine day. Chithra and I talked about sharing the driving, taking turns every three hours, but I ended up doing most of it anyway. On the third day, driving through a forest, we came upon a rusty old signboard to a temple. There were a few people near the signboard, and they seemed to be waiting for a bus. I stopped the car and asked for directions. They pointed down the forest path. One of the men, speaking in broken English, said that the temple was about a kilometre down that road, and that we could drive down for a fair distance. This was not a big forest, he said, there were no elephants or tigers here, but he cautioned us to be careful when getting out of the car and walking around, as there were plenty of cobras. He did not know what the deity at the temple was. A forest god, he said, at least that is what people believed.

We drove down the path. After driving for three quarters of a kilometre, we caught sight of it. A small temple nestled among big trees, some of which I easily identified—peepal, champak, wood apple, neermaruthu. Those trees brought back memories of the forest and the little dilapidated kaavu in Eranmoola.

I stopped the car when it became difficult to drive on further. As we got out of the car, we saw a family walking toward us from the temple. They looked like Malayalis, and we struck up a conversation. They were from the Thrissur area, the husband a retired professor and the wife an agricultural officer. His father-in-law, son, daughter-in-law and grandson made up the rest of the group.

'It's a good temple,' said the Professor. 'Very peaceful atmosphere.'

'The prasadam is tender coconut,' his wife added with a smile. 'Isn't that strange? This doesn't look like a place where coconut trees grow, and yet . . . I wonder how that custom came to be.'

'Perhaps there is some old Malayali connection,' said the Professor.

He was right about the atmosphere. It felt peaceful. The temple and surroundings brought to mind the small temples back home, where local deities were worshipped. The only difference was that the courtyard was paved with big blocks of granite and the temple compound had a waist-high wall around it.

Chithra dropped a hundred-rupee note in the collection box and, as if to rationalize her action, said, 'It's such a good thing that this temple is being maintained in the middle of this forest.'

'I'm sure they make enough money through donations to maintain a priest and a couple of helpers,' I said. I didn't think Chithra liked my reply.

We moved toward the entrance of the sanctum. I stood aside until Chithra and the others finished their prayers. When it was my turn, I moved forward and the priest stepped aside to allow me a full view of the idol. All I could see was a strange statue sculpted out of granite, with no recognizable marks to say which god or goddess it represented. I placed a ten-rupee note on the holy steps, and extended my cupped palms for prasadam. The priest reached into the darkness in front of the idol and brought out a tender coconut, the top of which was neatly carved into a wide mouth. He dipped a spoon into its mouth and poured the water into my palms, ritually—three times. I looked up at the priest. It was Mohanan! The tender coconut seller from Kudungomkaavu! It had been many years since I last saw him, but I knew I wasn't mistaken. It was him. But there was no change in his expression. No consternation, no glimmer of recognition, nothing. I couldn't take my eyes off him and stood rooted to the spot and, perhaps because of it, Mohanan dipped his spoon once again inside the coconut. Once more, its water fell into my cupped palms. The mildly cold, sweet water of the tender coconut.

Ilaneer, 2015

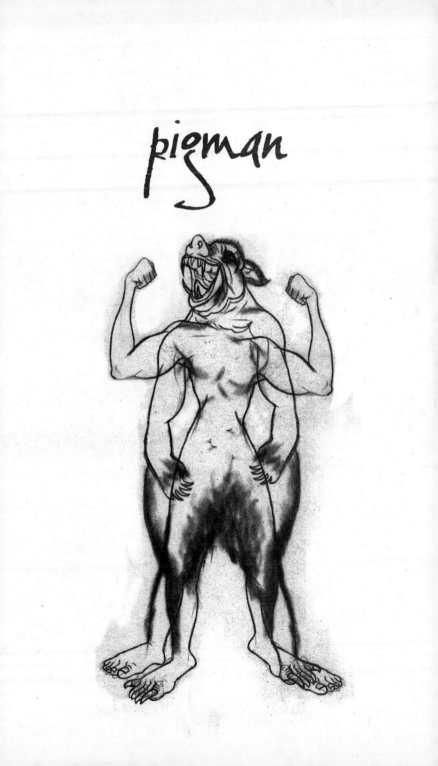

Sreekumar has gone back to his village. His father and brother-in-law came to take him home. Before he left, he took me aside and gave me this notebook. I accepted it without asking him what it was, or why he was giving it to me.

This is not a diary or a story. It's not quite a memoir either. To be honest, I am not sure what to call this narrative. Whatever it is, it is clear that Sreekumar did not intend to keep it private—on the very first page, he has written: 'To be read by all.' The notes are written in simple English in his beautiful handwriting. All I am doing is rendering his words into Malayalam.

I don't think you'd be too bored when you read this narrative, even if you know nothing about Sreekumar. Still, I want to exercise the privilege of the translator and record a few things by way of an introduction.

I live in room 21 on the first floor of the Research Scholars' Hostel. Sreekumar was in the room next to mine. I was in the sociology department and he was in linguistics.

We had been neighbours for over two years, but we'd barely spoken to each other in all that time. There was no disagreement or enmity between us. It's just that Sreekumar was somewhat reserved by nature. Besides, that's how things work around here—except for an occasional smile or a look of acknowl-edgement, most people mind their own business and don't get involved with others. Life on this campus seems to be defined by an almost obsessive self-love and an irrational dislike for others.

Still, occasionally, small groups congregate in the canteen or at the student centre or the guest house and engage in dis-cussions on a variety of topics: the off-stage manipulations for the next vice chancellor post, the altercations between a pro-fessor and a reader in some department, the castes of syndicate members, the possible legal angles to use in order to challenge someone's appointment. I never saw Sreekumar take part in these discussions. He didn't make friends, didn't speak much to anyone, and seemed totally uninterested in the goings-on in the campus. I gathered that it was best to leave someone so intensely private alone and never tried to initiate a friendship.

Two months ago, a colleague, Philip Mathew, told me a story. Philip had spent the evening in the city with some friends, engaging in some serious drinking. It was late when he got back to the campus, almost two o'clock in the morning. As he walked in, he caught sight of a man with a hat and a stick standing in front of the hostel. Puzzled, he rubbed his eyes and looked again. It was Sreekumar from Linguistics!

'Hello, what are you doing here at this time of the night?' he called out.

Sreekumar said, 'The watchman has a difficult job to do. I would've packed it in a long time ago if only I could find some other job.'

Something was not quite right here, Philip thought. He assumed that Sreekumar must be high on ganja or charas or some other drug and put the incident out of his mind.

A few days later, Philip was working on a seminar paper when he heard a noise. Looking out of his window, he saw Sreekumar chasing after something in the bushes. Again, he was wearing a hat.

Philip told me this story the day after that incident, when we were on our way to the university office. Since then, I too began watching Sreekumar. I couldn't find anything obviously wrong with his behaviour. It was only later that I came to know that he had stopped going to the department, that he spent his time wandering around. He had failed to file his progress report and the authorities had suspended his scholarship. He owed two months' payment at the students' mess. I don't know who informed his family. In the end, they came to the campus and he went away with them.

I know nothing about his family or personal circumstances, except that he was from some hillside village in Kannur district. I've heard that he wrote poetry occasionally. The rest, I have guessed. He was always in financial difficulties and felt a certain sense of inferiority because of that.

This is all I know about Sreekumar. I have not edited or interfered with these notes in any way.

Just one more thing before I stop. I have my own doubts about what I said at the beginning: Is this actually a story? If it isn't, what exactly is it?

Current consensus seems to be that these are the days of the reader and not of the author. If that is true, you have the right to come to your own conclusions.

What you will read next are Sreekumar's own words.

12 July 1994, Tuesday

Today is one of the most important days of my life.

I grew up in great hardship. Pursued my studies with no particular aim, finally ending up with a masters degree in linguistics. After that, I spent four or five years in the fruitless search for a job. The indignities, hurt and adversity I faced in that time . . . Oh . . . thinking of those days still makes me shudder.

But today, all of that feels like ancient history. Today, I feel as if I have overcome all my problems in a single leap. After all, the human mind is a fickle thing.

As of 10 AM this morning, I am a junior accountant at the head office of the Greatway Pig Farm. I am one of twelve new employees to join this institution today. All we were required to do on our first day was to sign the register. Our real jobs start tomorrow, after the managing director's address to the new employees.

Tonight, I am staying at a hotel—Hotel Orpheus—which charges fifty rupees per night. The hotel and its surroundings are extremely dirty.

It was a clear day until the evening, when there was a downpour which stopped as suddenly as it started. But now, it is raining quite heavily, its sound assaults my ears like the relentless roar of some feral creature.

In a couple of days, I will move. People like me cannot afford to stay in a place like this for long. The first year is the probation period, with a monthly salary of 1,250 rupees. Only after that they will decide on a salary scale and other benefits.

I picked up this pen wanting to write something nice about life. I have failed. Words are the problem. If you are in possession of a good vocabulary, you will have a good life. Is that a fact? I don't know. It's just a thought that came to me and I have written it down. That's all. Anyway, I am happy today. My mind is at peace. Thank you, Greatway Pig Farm, thank you!

13 July 1994, Wednesday

The managing director, Suman Shastri, bade us—eight men and four women—a hearty welcome to Greatway Pig Farm and spoke to us for precisely fifteen minutes. We were given an abstract of his presentation beforehand.

We were told that, during the probation period, we had to be ready and willing to do any job around the farm, regardless of our position. Even if you were appointed as an artist in the advertising department, you had to learn to pitch in with feeding the pigs.

Greatway has farms in Bihar, Andhra Pradesh, Kerala, Karnataka and Tamil Nadu—a total of 600 acres of land. In addition to the pig farms, they own tourist homes in Kullu and Darjeeling. The company's ambition is to diversify into the newspaper and fashion industries next.

Greatway raises Berkshire pigs on their farms. This is a type of pig that is quite popular in pig farms in England, Australia and New Zealand. A full grown male weighs anywhere between 275 and 375 kilograms.

The company has invested in everything that is required for successful pig farming. The pigs are housed in clean sheds with plenty of light and air. Each farm has qualified workers with specialist training in tending to pigs, and a veterinarian on call. The company expects careful, attentive and dedicated service from all its employees.

Almost 900 tonnes of pork reaches the markets daily from Greatway. Pork retails at 35 to 40 rupees a kilo these days, but the company sells it to wholesalers for a mere 25 rupees. Three years ago, when the company started trading, it had a market value of 16.8 crore rupees. Today, its shares are trading at 38 rupees and experts predict that this will increase to 45 rupees within a short period. That's how much confidence the market has in the company.

Greatway has pledged to make the country self-sufficient in meat production. The employees are expected to work hard to ensure that the shareholders' interests are safe with the company. The company will entertain no compromise in this matter.

22 July 1994, Friday

Greatway's head office is housed in a beautiful building shaped like a Tibetan temple. It stands in the middle of the ninety-acre farm, attracting the attention of everyone who sees it. The path leading up to it is made of fine sand and, on either side of the path, potted plants have been used to create a veritable magical land of many scents and colours. Three months ago, when I came here for my interview, I had goosebumps thinking about working in this environment.

It has only been a few days, and how my attitude has changed!

This strange world I am now part of is creeping me out. To the extent that, sometimes, I find myself questioning the reality of what I do here and what is happening around me.

My current responsibility is to keep an accurate record of the numbers and weights of the pigs being sent to the market every day. The trucks arrive to fetch the pigs usually around 3 PM. It goes on until 5 PM and sometimes even after that.

Until this work starts, I am expected to spend time in the farm. We have to learn all aspects of pig farming by observing and interacting with the farm workers. We are expected to demonstrate personal initiative and be proactive in this for the first three months.

I've already learned a lot about the sows. A perfect sow is one that has a voluptuous and fleshy body, and a calm temperament. Sows begin to show signs of the desire to mate when they are about five or six months old. When a female starts mounting other females in the group with a peculiar grunting noise, it is an indication that she is in heat. But it is better to wait for another couple of months before allowing her to mate, so that she produces healthy, hearty babies.

The male pigs are to be allowed to mate only twenty times a month. A male pig is, under no circumstance, to be allowed to mate as and when he pleases. If you do, he will overexert himself to a premature death.

I have already learned a lot of such things. Still, there are many things in the farm that I don't understand, and when I am in the office, this thought makes me anxious. I want to share my feeling of anxiety with someone, but I haven't found anyone suitable to confide in.

My interactions with my colleagues are limited to the few pleasantries we exchange. Everyone is busy with their work, and when they do have some free time, they tend to withdraw into their private worlds. People seem scared of developing anything other than a passing acquaintance with one another. Or perhaps they don't wish for anything more than that.

The office is shrouded in an insipid silence which is interrupted intermittently by the clatter of typewriters and, every time I listen to it, an inchoate fear sinks its teeth into my chest. I look up yearning for some kind of human connection, only to be met with heavy, brooding faces staring at the open files in front of them.

I have moved into a rented house which I share with three other employees from Greatway—a small bungalow on the hillside around three kilometres away from the farm. Apart from sharing a living space, we are alone here too. Jose, who is the storekeeper at the farm, immerses himself in his books—career guides, self-help books, quiz magazines. He is a disciplined young man, with big dreams and a great enthusiasm for life. The other two are Ashokan and Mukesh. As soon as he leaves the office, Ashokan takes off for the city, returning only in time for dinner and going to bed immediately after. Mukesh is still a mystery. He seems downcast most of the time, barely speaking and reluctant to even smile.

I am caught in an unbearable sense of loneliness, both at the office and at home. The only relief I have from this miserable existence is the time I spend with the farmhands. Thimma is the oldest among them—a tall, lean, middle-aged man. He was a servant at the managing director's house before he came to work at the farm. The MD had a small pig farm in those days, and Thimma was in charge of running it. Although he is much lower in the hierarchy here, Thimma is the kind of person who isn't submissive and speaks his mind to everyone, always with a pleasant and open face.

I think Thimma knows everything there is to know about the farm, the good and the bad, but he does not talk about any of it. The only subject that interests him is the pigs. Ask him anything about them and he will answer gladly and patiently, his face bright with enthusiasm. Facts about a pig's life from birth to death are at the tip of his tongue, each detail carefully preserved as though it were divine wisdom which he is ready to impart to anyone who asks.

Thimma does not have a home of his own, or any relatives or friends outside the farm. He spends all his time here, loving and nurturing the pigs, male and female, young and old. As they are dragged by ropes around their necks and loaded on to trucks, Thimma tries to soothe them, stroking their bodies one last time. The pigs scream; they know that they are being taken away to their death. Their piercing cries echo around the farm.

And when the last of the trucks departs, Thimma looks at me, his eyes red and puffy. I look away.

I am not knowingly committing any sin. I am just doing my job. Besides, the person responsible for the sins we commit as human beings is God. He is the one who gives life, nurtures it or destroys it.

26 July 1994, Tuesday

I received a letter from my mother today. This is the third letter Amma has written since I started this job. As usual, the letter is full of random news; the real reason for the letter is revealed only at the end.

'Your father's behaviour has deteriorated since you left. He is always angry. The amount of money he spends in the toddy shop is unbelievable. I don't dare say anything. I am scared of what he might do.

'Suma has a marriage proposal. The boy is working in the Gulf. You might know him—Kuniyankunnil Shankaran Maistry's son, Divakaran. He won't get leave to come home for another three months. He sent his brother, brother-in-law and another person to come and see Suma. I simply have no idea what to do about the expenses. How can we get her married off to a man working in the Gulf without giving at least fifteen pavan of gold? Your father doesn't care. Only you can make this happen. I don't have anyone else except you.'

Normally, such a letter would have worried me. But today, I feel nothing. Achchan, Amma, Suma, they are all so far away. I feel as if I am in an entirely different world that they cannot even comprehend.

Something significant has happened to my mind, but I cannot muster up the energy or interest to understand what it is.

27 July 1994, Wednesday

'Pigman'—this construction is possible. There must be such a word in some dialect of the English language. At the very least, someone must have used it in a story or a poem.

29 July 1994, Friday

The pigs were not let out of the sheds today. It has been raining heavily since morning. The piercing wind cuts through the bones, freeze-drying the body. In the sheds, in their hay beds, perhaps the pigs don't feel this intense cold.

15 August 1994, Monday

At 8.30 this morning, all the farm employees assembled in front of the office. After hoisting the national flag, the MD gave a short speech praising the great souls who had dedicated their lives to the Independence struggle, and expressing his hope that their bravery and sacrifice would be an example for us. He highlighted the contributions Greatway was continuing to make toward the good of the country. The current value of our stock was thirty-nine rupees, he said, and asked us to work harder than ever to increase the public's confidence in the company. He told us that Greatway was poised to make its entry into the publishing world, and ended his speech by assuring us that the company was well-placed to meet its goals through disciplined hard work.

19 August 1994, Friday

The farm has acquired around 200 Yorkshire Large Whites. Impressive beasts, with broad bodies and without the sunken faces of the Berkshires. They have a kind of majesty in their bearing.

20 August 1994, Saturday

The MD is at the farm only for five or six days a month. He spends the rest of the time at farms in other states, or travelling on company business. The administrative officer, Veeraswami, who is in charge when the MD is not around, revels in sending ripples of fear around the farm. He seems to think that his main job is to abuse and bully people.

The sense of self-importance he tries to convey through his bearing and general demeanour does not fool anyone. Everyone knows that he is a lecherous womanizer. Every so often, he summons the women staff into his cabin. There are those who are eager to be summoned and go in with a smile, others who get up from their seats with a resigned look on their faces, and yet others who clearly show their disgust when they hear their names being called. Their faces are suffused with these different expressions when they return to their seats after ten or twenty minutes. The male staff don't seem to pay much attention and seem to have accepted this as a routine part of affairs.

Today, after lunch at around 2 PM, the AO summoned me to his office. I usually meet with him at ten past ten in the morning and submit the previous day's transactions, details about the weights and numbers of pigs, give brief answers to his queries and sign the daily accounts register. I felt uneasy as soon as I heard him call me at this unusual hour. I had so far managed to avoid his abuse, and my heart raced as I walked into his cabin.

Veeraswami stared at me for a couple of minutes, and asked, 'Have you never seen women before?'

'Yes, sir.'

'So what is this that I hear?' He raised his voice. 'Why have you been ogling at her?'

Completely lost for words, I just stood there perspiring.

'Get out, you dirty pig,' he thundered.

As I staggered out of his office in shock, I saw all my colleagues hide their laughter behind their hands.

23 August 1994, Tuesday

There have been some changes to my duties.

From now on, my job is to keep track of pig feed—maize, barley, wheat chaff, etc.—and the remains from the abattoir. I am not quite sure if this change is meant to be a punishment.

Thimma told me, 'Look on the bright side. At least now you are saved from accounting for the animals as they go to their deaths.'

24 August 1994, Wednesday

I had a terrible nightmare last night. An enormous pig, as big as an elephant, was eating me. I woke up screaming, 'Who's done this? Who is it that fed me to the pig?'

25 August 1994, Thursday

A sense of anxiety has enveloped Greatway. A new farm, Whiteway, has started its operations in Assam and is said to have considerable investment and backing. Their head office is in Guwahati, and they have already bought 300 acres of land in Uttar Pradesh and Bihar. Word is that they have financial investment from the famous Canadian farm, Greenland.

The pigs at Whiteway are Yorkshire Whites, but of the medium type. Since they reach maturity faster, they are less expensive to farm and their meat is of a better quality than the Large Whites.

Hotcake, a magazine that mixes news about the meat industry with pornographic content, has published a write-up about Whiteway, alongside an advertisement announcing job openings across the company. They are offering a better salary scale and additional benefits, and the ad says that preference will be given to people with previous experience in the industry.

I don't know who brought that copy of *Hotcake* into the office. People grabbed it off each other's hands, trying to get a look at it and, by the afternoon, the atmosphere in the office had changed. The air felt lighter and people more congenial. In the canteen, there were loud discussions about the possibilities opened up by Whiteway, each person finding something favourable to say: how the Medium Yorkshire Whites were more suited to the Indian environment, their high productivity, the significance of the company's financial collaboration with Greenland, and so on.

26 August 1994, Friday

When I went into the AO's cabin this morning, he seemed anxious. After the excitement yesterday, my colleagues also seemed subdued and tense.

I am not worried about what might happen to Greatway. I will continue working here and be part of the company until they fire me. What happens after that? I am not quite ready to think about that yet.

31 August 1994, Wednesday

Ever since I came here, I have not read a single book. The couple of books I had brought with me lie on the table, covered in dust. I just can't bring myself to open them. I wouldn't mind getting my hands on some porn, but I don't seem to be able to muster up the energy to read anything serious.

I wish I could begin an entry like this: 'There was a girl in my life. Her name was . . .' It would be true, but it would also be a joke. The peaks and waves of romantic love—they seem otherworldly.

Last night, I became a wild tree of lust. A tree that grew as tall as the sky. All night, dew fell on it, drenching its leaves and branches, and even its taproot.

9 September 1994, Friday

The farm's supervisor Thankayya and senior accountant

Shashankan have gone to Guwahati. They got an interview call from Whiteway.

But that was not the news that shocked the farm today. Six of our pigs have died. Each of them developed a high fever, throat pain, blood in the urine, redness of ears and shivering, and died within six hours of exhibiting these symptoms. I will never forget the image of Thimma and the vet, Doctor Daniel, sitting numb beside their dead bodies.

In the evening, there was an emergency meeting of the entire staff, which everyone except Thimma attended. Veeraswami told us that it was part of normal farm affairs that some pigs would become ill and die. He implored us not to give it undue significance, and warned us not to talk about the incident to anyone outside. After his speech was over, a couple of people took him up on his offer to ask questions. What exactly had caused the pigs' death—that's what they wanted to know. They had died of anthrax, said Veeraswami, adding that the company had already sent for anti-anthrax serum.

It was 6 PM by the time the meeting adjourned. I waited until everyone left and, deciding that it was better to walk rather than wait for the bus, I set out down the road that ran along the farm's boundary. I looked around, as if seeing the sparsely populated valley and the surrounding hills for the first time. It was an extraordinary landscape, where eternity kissed the tips of my fingers. In the fading light, unsettling thoughts sprouted and an ancient sadness welled up deep in my mind. I turned the corner and began descending the hill. Darkness descended with me.

In the dimly lit yard of the arrack shop by the road, a small crowd had assembled, the men almost naked, the women in tattered dark saris and the shrivelled children with frizzy hair. The crowd weaved back and forth, laughing uproariously. I thrust myself into the crowd and strained to see whatever was unfolding.

In the middle of the yard, surrounded by the crowd, was Thimma. He was on all fours, his face down, nose rooting in the dust. Wearing only a pair of sweat-stained black underpants, he wobbled his body and moved around, grunting. That body covered in black dust, that wobbly movement—that was not the Thimma I knew. That was a filthy country swine.

I strained forward, wanting to stop him, but I couldn't move. My legs were rooted in the mud, shins heavy and swollen.

10 September 1994, Saturday

Thimma is dead. He started exhibiting the exact symptoms that the pigs had. Several people begged Veeraswami to take him to the hospital, but he paid no heed to their appeals.

Thimma died lying on a bed in front of the shed used to house castrated piglets.

Speaking to each one of us individually, Veeraswami warned us not to talk about the incident to anyone outside the farm.

At dusk, we dug a hole under a big tree in the northern corner of the farm and buried Thimma. Apart from the farmhands, it was just me and Veeraswami. I tried not to cry but failed.

11 September 1994, Sunday

Thoughts churn. Without words to moor them, they circle like leaves and twigs caught in a whirlpool. I have become a throbbing ache.

14 September 1994, Wednesday

Thousands of pigs at the farm have died. Our main job now is burying their carcasses in deep pits lined with lime. The sheds are washed with disinfectant in the morning and evening, and yet the smell of rotting pig meat seems to permeate the atmosphere.

The city newspaper's evening edition had a long report about the illness that has afflicted Greatway's pigs. It was not anthrax or swine plague, it said, but a new type of viral infection. The insinuation was that this virus was developed in Whiteway's labs for the specific purpose of annihilating Greatway farms. Another North Indian newspaper had already published a report along these lines.

Pigs have started dying in Greatway's farm in Bihar since yesterday. There is no hope for a quick cure for this new virus, a fact that is upsetting the employees and everyone else associated with Greatway. The shareholders who had invested tens of thousands of rupees in Greatway are beside themselves. 'The disaster that has befallen this company after three consecutive years of financial progress is something that hurts everyone,' said the report in conclusion.

19 September 1994, Monday

Another letter from Amma . . .

'Why didn't you come home for Onam, my son? Please write soon, I will worry until I hear from you.

'Divakaran will be coming home next month. His brother says he has two months' leave but we'll have to hurry up with the wedding. Chandrettan said he'll give Suma two bangles, and Damodaran has offered to take care of the wedding ring. Now if we can retrieve the pawned ornaments from the bank, the jewellery issue will be solved. The sooner the better, so we'll have enough time to get them remade according to Suma's wishes. You must try to help and get this done.'

I bought an inland letter and wrote back: 'I couldn't get away for Onam, too much work here. I'll be home by the 30th. Don't worry about the pawned jewellery. I'll get it back as soon as I am home.'

I didn't feel sad when I posted the letter. It is better to postpone news that will cause unnecessary hurt to others. Even if it is for another ten days—even for an hour.

20 September 1994, Tuesday

Re-reading these notes I've kept since I came to Greatway, it seems odd that I have not written anything at all about the salary I've received so far. The 1,250 rupees I received on 2 August is the first salary I have ever received in my entire life. But I felt no special emotion about it. I sent off a hundred rupees each to Achchan, Amma and Suma immediately.

Often, I find the things that other people consider significant in their lives to be irrelevant. Who knows—perhaps I am the one with the right attitude.

21 September 1994, Wednesday

A pig farm on the brink of utter ruin. An insignificant man still clinging on to it. A written account of his thoughts and experiences has nothing really to contribute to human culture. How I wish I could write about things that would move beyond these ordinary narratives. But my mind is empty. Not even pigs range there.

Undated

All through its life, the pig walks with its head lowered, looking downward. A beating with an iron rod or a stick, a stomach pierced with a spear, or some other means picked by man—its death is certain. And at the precise moment of its death, it raises its face to the sky for the first time. Poor thing! It dies with the knowledge that the sky, after all, is empty.

Undated—A Dream

I've arrived at a hillside. I've travelled far.

I cannot go any further. It's a dead end. It's empty and still here. There is not even the flicker of a shadow. A threatening silence cloaks everything like mist.

Suddenly, I see a broken sign—'Greatway Pig Farm'. Still, I have to search for a while before I see the gate to the farm. It lies open. I enter.

This farm is not the one I am familiar with. On both sides of the path, pig-trotters bloom out of dirt holes. Behind them, a row of dilapidated sheds and, beyond them, leafless trees.

Finally, I reach the office—the same office I go to every day. Yellow lights shine inside, but there is no one around. The front door to the office is open. With a trembling heart, I enter, looking this way and that. No, there is no one around. In the dim yellow light, the wide hall lies empty. I turn to leave.

'Hello.' Someone calls me from behind. I turn around and see a man. He is naked, white and shimmering from head to toe. He extends his hand toward me and, as if in some kind of stupor, I also extend mine. He comes running toward me, shakes my hand and then embraces me. Suddenly, shockingly,

I realize that the hand that shook mine is actually the trotter of a pig.

I am not quite sure how I do it, but I shake him off. With a queer laugh, he turns and walks away from me.

He walks away on all fours, wagging the dirty stub of his tail, and sticking his naked butt out toward me.

Pigman, 1994

invisible forests

'The sky is just the sky,' Krishna told herself silently as she sat in the bus, the next instant thinking, 'I should have said, "The sky is not just the sky."' Words were what kept her alive. From ten o'clock in the morning until one in the afternoon, and then again from 2 PM until four or five in the evening, she talked, loudly and non-stop, to her students. In the bus to work and back, and alone in her attic room at home, she talked silently to herself or to an imagined other. On the rare holidays when Shantha or Shyamedathi came to visit, she enveloped them in a blanket of words. The only time she didn't talk was when she was with the other members of her family.

Krishna had no degree or qualifications in the two subjects—history and literature—she taught at Chethana Parallel College. But neither her students nor the principal, Gopakumar, seemed to care. 'Nobody here is going to know that the teacher has no formal qualifications in these subjects,' Gopakumar had told her on her first day. And, as if revealing a great truth, he'd continued, 'You are a lecturer now. Your job is to lecture. A lecture means an assemblage of words.'

Krishna had thought then that he was an intelligent and entertaining man. It was only later that she realized that, beyond his fancy words and turns of phrases, he was just another boring schemer.

It was unusually late when she left Chethana that evening. The staff meeting that had started at 4.30 PM dragged on until after six, the discussions about salary arrears and vacation pay reaching nowhere. Gopakumar told them that he was in debt—to the tune of 150,000 rupees. He promised them that it would not affect their salaries. He said, in a voice trembling with emotion, that he would pay them all even if he had to sell the ten cents of land he owned in town. Sitting in the bus, Krishna thought about his words and gestures but did not dwell on their sincerity.

She got off the bus at Cheriyangadi. As she walked past the deserted market and turned on to the dirt road toward home, she looked up at the darkening sky. 'The sky is something like a sky,' she said.

2.

'People don't ask for permission when they fall in love.'

Sitting up in her bed in the middle of the night, Krishna told Dileepan, 'I was always so aware of you—your serious face, the surefooted way you walked, the twinkle in your eyes, the thickness of your moustache . . . I knew you were smart, intellectually much superior to the other boys, which is why I kept my distance. Your college debates and speeches were full of ideas too lofty for my own intellectual capabilities. My interests, in those days, were trivial, ordinary. Joseph was the right person to share those interests with. It's only now that I realize I could have shared them with you too. Well, there is no point in dwelling on that now, nothing to gain by worrying about what could have been.

'You've only spoken to me once or twice. One time, we sat next to each other for an essay competition on environmental issues. You got the first prize and I got the second. That could have been an opportunity to get to know each other better, but it didn't happen.

'When you came here last month in connection with your research, it was the first time we'd met since our college days. I was so glad that you remembered me. I don't remember telling you that this was where I lived. We didn't have the kind of relationship that would have prompted such an exchange of personal information—we weren't even in the same class. Still, you remembered.

'I know I didn't ask you much about your research project. Something to do with wild plants, I gathered that much. I came with you to Poothakkavu, the woods near my house, where you pottered around for a long time. When we were children, my friends and I used to spend most of our holidays in those woods. How lush it used to be, with so many varieties of trees, vines and flowering bushes. In the middle of the woods, there used to be a pond, a small one, but it had water even in the driest summer. The woods were full of sun berries, fox cucumbers, thirippan kaaya. Bird nests, nimble-footed mongoose and rabbits, the whispers of snakes . . . A long-ago time of endless wonders.

'As I grew up, I forgot about the woods. An entire world right next door slowly grew alien and far away.

'The woods have changed too, as time passed. They've shrunk and lightened as the venerable old trees disappeared, vines fell to the ground to wither and die, and the bounty of flowers ended. Still, the woods persist in the trees and plants no one wants, in the seasonal renewal of grass, and in the birds and butterflies unaffected by their lonely abandonment.

'So, when I came with you to the woods, it was the first time in years I'd been there. I chatted, non-stop, as you wandered around examining the weeds and shoots, smelling and pinching at them. I feel embarrassed thinking about it now, how I jabbered on without waiting for a response from you, drunk from the joy of seeing you again, from being able to spend time with you. It is quite unlike me, this chatter, you must have thought. But I am sure that you didn't find it distasteful. You'd changed too, in the last seven or eight years. Your face had lost its sober expression—you seemed more relaxed, easy-going. Younger, somehow. The dark blue shirt and faded brown trousers you had on suited you.

'There were changes in the way you behaved too. You thought I wasn't paying attention, didn't you, given my non-stop patter? Oh, but I was quite conscious of the way you looked at me, where your eyes fell on my body, and the way you quickly averted them when I interrupted one such look. Thinking about it now, I feel good. You are the reason I have a new urge to love this body once again, to run my fingers tenderly along its curves and shadows. And you are so completely unaware of it.

'After you left, my father scolded me. "Research and college and all that is one thing," Achchan told me. "You're a woman, remember that. You've already done enough to set tongues wagging. Don't set them off again. There's nothing wrong with this family, and yet you've not been able to find yourself a husband. Whose fault do you think that is?" He went on for quite some time. Usually, Achchan does not allow himself the freedom or familiarity to scold us. Something got to him that day.

'Listening to him, I did not feel sad but angry. There are only two male members who are a regular part of this household—Achchan and Dasettan. And I know them well. Neither one of them would be able to face the questions I have for them—they'd disappear like smoke. I know all about them. The reason I hold my tongue is because I don't want to upset anyone. But I won't be intimidated. You should come again, whenever you can, and I will happily come along with you to any forests or hills, show you the kind of flowers and trees you have never seen before.

'I think you came to my home and to Poothakkavu because of your love for me. Your research was the cause, that's all. I'd like to believe so, even if it isn't true. True love is not just about physical attraction. It requires a particular mindset and intelligence. You have both. True love! It is like a ghost. Everyone has heard of it and has lots to talk about it, but only very few have come across it face-to-face. I'm sure someone else would have said something like this about love. Don't you think so? Well, if they haven't, consider this an original contribution from me.

'Tonight, there is one thought that is disturbing me. I asked you so many questions about your life, but never asked whether you were married. Perhaps I was avoiding asking that question. Perhaps I was hoping for something I didn't deserve, beyond this love of ours. I don't know . . .'

3.

'Shyamedathi, I'll be honest with you. I only took the membership because you insisted. I have no intention of coming to your meetings.'

'Is it because you're scared of your father?'

'No.'

'Well, you don't have to worry about that. It was your uncle Ravi who asked me to make you a member. I don't think Chandutti Mooppar will object to something Ravi approves of.'

'What did Ravimaman say to you?'

'Only good things. He told me and Kausu several times that we should get you involved in the Association. Get you to be active.'

'Is Maman looking to be a candidate for the elections?'

'Why would you ask that, Krishna?'

'I mean, I'm just wondering why he has this sudden interest in me.'

'Rubbish. He's always cared about your well-being.'

'Right. Well, he did try quite hard to get me married off. And, of course, he's the one who got me the job at Gopan's college. That's not what I meant. The Party and Association have been going on for a while, no? I just wondered why he never thought of getting me involved until now.'

'Does that mean he can't think of it now? And what possible impact would your joining the Association have on his election prospects?'

'Well, if he is looking for candidacy, he might be feeling especially motivated.'

'It's the Party who chooses the candidate.'

'Yes, but Maman is a big shot in the Party, isn't he?'

'There are no such hierarchies in the Party.'

'Of course there are. Can you, Shyamedathi, get things done in the Party in the same way that he can?'

'What do you want from me, Krishna? Do you want to

argue with me and shut me up? I'm happy to give in, just as long as you come to the meeting on Tuesday.'

'What would be the point? I have no intention of taking part in your debates and discussions. No interest whatsoever in being a leader.'

'Well, even if you were interested, that's not going to happen.'

'Not until I butter up all the big shots, right?'

'Stop being flippant, Krishna.'

'Do you really think I'm being flippant, Shyamedathi? Come on, you can be honest, it's just the two of us here.'

'You're just trying to wriggle out of coming to the meeting.'

'Maybe so. Still, do you really think I'm wrong? Take Sulochana, for example—Advocate Rajan's wife. How long has she been part of the Women's Association? And how long have you been working for the Party? What contribution has she made to get to be a panchayat member? Sulochana is rich. She has money, and posh clothes and jewellery. And Rajan is well-connected with the leaders of the Party. She is where she is because of these things, and not because she's ever been involved in a hunger strike or been beaten by the police or helped the poor.'

'Krishna, don't get sucked into gossip.'

'It's not gossip though, is it? How many people in the Party have the guts to speak up when Sulochana does something wrong? None. All the budding leaders will clamp up because they are scared of Advocate Rajan.'

'Yes, well, when you are on the outside it is easy to form such opinions. Try getting involved if you want to know what's what.'

'Actually, I think those who are on the outside have a better insight.'

'Believe what you want, but please come to the meeting. We are determined to take on the proliferation of illegal liquor and the spreading alcohol problem within this Panchayat. We are going to discuss setting up squad work in each ward.'

'You think women can put an end to illegal hooch and the alcohol problem?'

'Why not? Imagine how good it would be if we were successful. In the 7th ward alone, there are at least a dozen full-time drunkards. You know what goes on in their homes.'

'Well, men will find something else to do if they have to give up drinking.'

'You're enjoying this, aren't you? This tit-for-tat. You've always been like this. As if I don't know you and your ways!'

'You're right about that, Shyamedathi. I like arguing with people. But you know who is better at arguing than I am? Ravimaman.'

'That was before. These days, he's very careful with his words. Have you heard any of his recent speeches? Such clarity of thought.'

'And yet you folk won't give him the chance to be an MLA.'

'Well, the Party will make those decisions when the time is right. Obviously, we can't send all our leaders to the Assembly, can we?'

'But Maman still holds on to that dream. That's the only reason he is still involved.'

'In your opinion.'

'I know him well, don't I? And I'll tell you one more thing.

Given the way things are, his dream will remain just that and it will be his own doing.'

'What do you mean?'

'Do you want me to spell it out for you, Shyamedathi?'

'I have no idea what you're going on about.'

'You don't? Then why were you smiling?'

'I didn't smile.'

'All right, you didn't smile. Maybe you don't know everything, but you do know that Devu's son got a job at the Cooperative Press?'

'So? What's wrong with that?'

'Nothing's wrong with it. No point being a leader of the Party if he can't use that privilege to find a job for someone close to him, right?'

'How in the world do you know all this?'

'Ah, the secret wheeling and dealing within the Party . . .'

'She's a tart, that Devu. She's the one who's led your uncle astray.'

'He's no saint himself. Besides, if Devu and Maman have something going on, it's not the end of the world, is it? He's never been married and she's a widow. Why should the Party care if they have a relationship?'

'Of course it cares! It cares very much if one of its leaders comes to disrepute.'

'So you're also against it, then?'

'I'm not for or against anyone.'

'As long as he's still a member, no one will say anything publicly. But the moment he's out of the Party, the naming and shaming will start.'

'Every party has its own disciplinary procedures.'

'But why such discipline only in these matters? Why not in other things that your comrades are involved in? Everyone is fully committed to promoting their own interests.'

'Oh, I've heard it all before. No one has anything to say about all the good stuff the Party does.'

'So you admit there's bad stuff too . . .'

'Wherever people come together, there's always good stuff and bad stuff. It's not the Party's fault.'

'Dasettan's party is also the same, although it's supposed to be Gandhi's party.'

'You're joking, aren't you? You think the Congress today is the party Gandhi set up? It's a bunch of thieves and liars. That's their politics.'

'But Dasettan is not interested in the Congress Party for its politics. His interest is in some of its members. Lillykutty teacher and Kamalam, for example.'

'For goodness sake, Krishna! Think before you speak. He's your brother-in-law after all.'

'So? Being Vimalechi's husband doesn't stop him from being who he is.'

'Hmm, I agree he's weird. No sense of decency.'

'Would you say that if he was in your party, Shyamedathi?'

'Our party won't put up with people like him.'

'I hear the Congress is also fed up with him . . .'

'Really?'

'He's got some new connections in the BJP. His current best mate is Kunnumbrath Unnikrishnan. The other day the two of them were sitting downstairs scolding the Mappilas.'

'Well, Congress supporters are usually quite friendly with the BJP lot.'

'Whatever. Being Dasettan's friend will only get them into trouble.'

'Still, how did Vimala end up doing such a stupid thing as marrying him? Your father and Ravimaman were both against it.'

'I can think of only one way out of it.'

'What's that?'

'Vimalechi should do exactly what he does. A woman has no difficulty finding a man if she's determined.'

'Goodness! How you say these things so easily! Why should she mess up her life just because her husband is a good-for-nothing?'

'Yeah, as if her life is so brilliant right now!'

'Well, she's getting on with it, isn't she, without making a song and dance about it?'

'Getting on with her life, yes. That, precisely, is the problem. All you party people and your associations think like that. You want a woman to remain in her place. Families, castes—everything has its place and should remain as it is. No revolutions allowed there!'

'What would you have us do, then? Interfere in people's personal affairs?'

'Each to their own, that's what you mean, isn't it? Everyone should put up with and take care of their own problems. If that's the case, what use are you lot?'

'I can't stand here and argue with you all day. I've got to go. Plenty to do.'

'Oh don't go, Shyamedathi. I was just mouthing off. Don't be upset.'

'Oh yeah, like I am so upset. If I were to be upset by what folks say, I'd have given this up long ago. Argue with me all you want, but see if I don't make you attend the meeting.'

'I can't see that happening.'

'We'll see.'

Shyamedathi left and a sudden feeling of exhaustion engulfed Krishna. She locked herself in her room and fell on her bed. After a while, she got up, picked up a notebook, and started writing in it—a note like a diary entry but without a date or time:

Today, Shyamedathi came to see me. She wanted me to become a member of the Women's Association. I had a long argument with her but, in the end, gave in and signed up. We had a long chat and gossiped about Ravimaman and Dasettan.

Shyamedathi is a good woman. She used to visit us all the time when Valliechi was at home. Now she doesn't come that often. She's very involved with the Party, but I feel that I still have the freedom to have an honest conversation with her. We've always had that openness. She will not accept any criticism of the Party, but doesn't get angry or upset with me even when I keep pushing the boundaries.

I may have gone a bit overboard today, I feel. I live an entirely self-centred life and, as such, have no right to criticize the Party or even to voice any opinion. I do absolutely nothing for others. Those who live like that have no business criticizing social action. My attack on Shyamedathi's party was purely based on the gossip I'd overheard in Chethana's staffroom. I was trying to get a rise out of her, just for fun.

Everyone else in Chethana is involved in politics. Gopan sir is an old Naxalite. He pretends to be a Marxist now, but he is scornful of their politics. Jitesh is the real Marxist, a minor leader of DYFI. Manoj's entire family supports the BJP and so does he, I think, deep inside, although he seems to be embarrassed to admit it publicly. So he pretends to be a radical and makes fun of all parties equally. Most of the quarrels in the staffroom are between Jitesh and Manoj. The others only pitch in with the occasional remark. As for me, I just sit back and enjoy the show. And when I am alone, I re-enact their words and voices. I find that highly entertaining.

I want to fill my mind with the clamour of words and voices all the time. Each time it is still, I feel silence growing like a forest inside me—a dense forest with thousands of forbidding animals and scuttling creatures.

4.

'Valliechi and Hariyettan arrive on Wednesday,' Krishna said, as though imparting the information to someone else.

'It's good that they're bringing Amala and Vineesh with them. Their cousins, Shanoj and Sarang, would have some reprieve from Vimalechi's incessant anger while they are here—she won't dare lose her temper around Valliechi's children.

'Those poor children! They bear the brunt of her anger toward Dasettan. She makes them sit with their books as soon as they are back from school. No going out, no watching TV . . . Why, they are not even allowed to spend time with me. I wonder what satisfaction she gets from taking out her frustrations on them, why she can't see how foolish and cruel it is.

'"This is not right," I said to her the other day. Oh, the way she reacted—scares me to think about it even now. She exploded as though I'd said something unspeakable. She stood there with her eyes bulging and mouth hanging open, the tendons on her neck taut, transformed into some other woman. I've never seen her like that before. Her words pelted me like stones, stunned me completely.

'That was the first time I cried since our mother's death. I was convinced that she'd suffered some kind of mental breakdown. I didn't talk about it to anyone except Shantha. What would be the point in that?

'Dasettan is beyond redemption. Vimalechi needs to understand what type of a man her husband is and, it seems to me, that she has only two choices: get rid of him, or adjust to his ways. But she seems incapable of doing either. So there is no solution to this situation. It consumes my sister like fire, and the smoke suffocates the children.

'There was a teacher named Philip who taught us psychology in college. He was a good teacher, but an alcoholic. I remember the time he came to the class fully drunk and said, "Psychology is a false science. It is nothing but a labyrinth of analysis. You never come out with a solution. Mental illness is the destiny of the mentally ill. The problems you face in your life are the result of that life—a life you have no control over, in which you have no choice. Even your choices are not of your own choosing.'"

5.

She was conscious of something like the sound of an oncoming storm rising inside her. Words rained, dark and torrential, in her mind.

On an afternoon soaked in rain, Krishna sat alone in her attic room and said to Jayamohan, 'I am not sure I understand what you mean. You're a socially conscious man and, as a journalist, you have a job that suits you. It allows you the freedom to think, say and write whatever you want. But I am not in that position, am I? Can I act on a freedom that I don't have? Can I go out and rent a house or a room in a lodge, and live independently? Will this society allow me to do that? Assure my safety?'

She stood up and sat down again. 'I know only one woman who has the courage to do any of this: Shantha. I don't think you know her. She is a friend of mine. We were classmates until class nine, when her father passed away and she had to drop out of school. She started going for daily wage work with her mother. Shantha is also unmarried, just like me. But she is not scared of anyone, doesn't care what people think of her, and lives exactly as she wants. She has always been gutsy, even when we were children.

'Shantha got pregnant when she was seventeen. She used to go to Abootty Haji's sawmill to collect sawdust, and there she got involved with his son, Salam. Salam was our school leader when we were in class eight. He was really handsome, with long soft hair, a shadow of a moustache and lovely rosy cheeks. Girls swooned when he smiled at them in his tucked-up mundu and handkerchief wristband. Shantha was also mesmerized, and would go to the corridor leading to the class ten room just to catch a glimpse of him.

'I guess she would have been over the moon to finally have the chance to get close to him. One time, during my pre-degree days, I was coming home from the college hostel for Onam holidays and ran into them at the bus stop. They'd just come out of Dr Shenoy's nursing home. Salam saw me and immediately said, "Ah good, you have company now," and left her with me and walked away.

'We were delayed as the driver had to pull the bus over along the way and wait for almost an hour to make space for a political rally. By the time we got off at our stop, it was dark. We'd shared a seat in the bus, but she hadn't said a single word to me—barely even looked at me—all the way.

'My father was waiting for me at the bus stop, and I wondered whether that was why she walked away without saying goodbye. But, the next morning, she came to see me. Sat right here in this room, and oh how she talked and cried. It was only then that I understood what had happened. In those days, I used to think these were horrible things, and was shocked to witness the intensity of her sorrow, scared that she'd lose her mind. But nothing happened. She got over it quite quickly. After Salam, there were others. Even now she has someone in her clutches—a contractor named Raju, a married man with two kids. Shantha has no compunction about such things. She still comes to see me whenever she can and tells me, unprompted, all about her relationships. She knows I am very interested in her stories. Sometimes I wonder whether she embellishes them a bit for my sake.

'Vimalechi and Ravimaman don't approve of our friendship. Vimalechi scolded me once for "letting that woman in our house." Vimalechi's concern is not about any wayward influence Shantha might have on her little sister. It is more about her husband, Dasettan, and his roving eyes. I feel so sorry for her. No matter what my sister does, that man is not going to change. If he thinks he's got a chance, he'll try anything with anyone. He even tried it with me once, but I put him in his place with one look. He thinks he is such a catch, but I find him revolting. Creeps like him will never be able to get me entangled in their nets.

'I know what you're thinking, Jayamohan. I know you're thinking, "But you got entangled in Joseph's net." You're mistaken. Yes we liked each other, and yes I've gone out with him—once to a coolbar and once to see a film. At the cinema hall, he put his arm around my shoulders and pulled me toward him, but when he tried to kiss me I didn't give in and covered my face with both my hands. That's all that's happened. And none of it is really important.

'Joseph forgot all about me and married into a rich family. Accepted a big dowry too. You all might think that he cheated me. That's not what I think. When we were together, his love for me was real. But love is not a contract. He never promised that he'd never marry anyone but me. In fact, we never even talked about marriage. I used to fantasize about spending time with him, but I don't think those fantasies included being his wife. Even if they did, I was careful to nip such thoughts in the bud. Are you wondering if that is indeed possible? It was, in my case, that's all I can say. Point is, I don't blame Joseph. When he left college, he took over the management of his father's furniture store. He made new connections and, when he had the opportunity, he used his marriage prospects to improve his circumstances. That's all.

'I'll admit that not everyone sees the world as I do. I hear people going on about how the world has changed, how our communities have grown psychologically. Why, even you wrote about it in today's newspaper. I disagree with that viewpoint. In my estimation, the world has not changed all that much. Granted, there have been some cosmetic changes, but deep inside people still retain the same regressive mindset. Why do you think the three marriage proposals I had didn't work out? Because some busybodies took it upon themselves to tell those families that I had a thing with a Christian boy while in college. To be honest, I was hurt when the first two proposals fizzled out. But with the third one, I was actually glad because I hadn't liked the prospective groom anyway.

'I turned thirty last December, and I don't think there will be any more proposals. Every month, for two or three days, my body feels strangely awash with an internal vibration. Still, I don't feel the least bit sorry that I might live out this life without the company of a man. I am quite capable of experiencing liberation and positive femininity—you know, the stuff you talk about constantly—on my own, without the help of a man. This thing I call my mind, it has developed certain capacities, and my body too is pretty skilled in tending to its own happiness.'

6.

'This used to be Venuvettan's room,' Krishna said, as though talking to Dileepan. 'When I moved in, the only thing that remained of him was a framed photograph. In it, he was a young boy, sitting on a wooden horse. It disappeared about eight or ten years ago. I asked Valliechi, and she said it might be in the wooden box in my father's room—a box in which Achchan had locked away all that remained of my brother.

'I was only three or four when Venuvettan left home. He had many radical friends and they often visited him at home. Among them was a man named Sahadevan, from Malappuram. My brother left home saying that he was going to see Sahadevan. Three days later, Valliechi received a letter from him. Many years later, she showed it to me; she has never shown it to any-one else. Its content is etched in my memory: "I'm not scared of death. I'm dedicating myself to the big battle. I know all of you might find it difficult to understand me, but I feel certain that history will vindicate my actions." What amazed me when I read that letter was not the conviction or bravery in those words, but the thought of him writing such words to his own sister. I wondered what sort of image he had of himself. Did he really believe that he'd become someone of significance and that history would remember him forever?

'I can only conclude that my brother got caught up in the idea that the version of himself that he'd conjured up with his words was who he really was—his true self. If that is true, I guess I too am in danger of being so foolish. I, too, am entrapped by words. All my thoughts emerge as self-contained sentences. I am bound by them entirely, constantly. Did I become like this because of my voracious reading habit, I wonder, and because I was into essay writing and debate competitions? I know now how foolish and meaningless such competitions are. People should speak or write when they really have something to share, not because they are required to. There should be no rules or misconceptions.

'I yearn for an existence where I am not constantly forming sentences, where my words don't stick to each other as though by some natural glue. Without some space between words to let in experiences, a person would suffocate.

'I am beginning to sound as though I'm saying something of significance. This yearning for significance, for greatness— this is my downfall. I don't know when the seed of this yearning was planted inside me, but I do know that it marked the beginning of my misfortune. It wasn't this apparent when we were still students. If it were, I wouldn't have become close to someone like Joseph instead of someone like you.

'I was telling you about Venuvettan. No one seems to have a clear idea about where he was or what he did for the few years after he left home. He doesn't seem to have made much of an impact even among the extremists. I've since read Ajitha's memoirs and a few essays on the Naxal Movement. There is no mention of a K.R. Venugopal in any of it.

'What we did hear was that, during the Emergency, he left Kerala and went to Andhra Pradesh and that, by the time he returned to Kerala, he'd become disillusioned with Naxal politics and was drinking heavily. No one from our family or our relatives saw him during this period. Eventually, one day, we got the news about his death: he had hung himself in a lodge room in Kozhikode.

'You can see the spot where he was cremated from this room—there, next to the aaval tree. I remember the crowd that had gathered, the noise, the explosion of our sorrow. I remember Amma rolling on the bare floor, senseless in her grief, Ravimaman and other relatives taking my shell-shocked Achchan inside the house. I remember how Valliechi wailed, holding on to me and Vimalechi. I can see it all, as if happening right now.

'All I really knew then, though, was that my older brother had died. Later, over a period of time, I heard many stories from many people. Initially, when I listened to them, all I felt was a natural sense of curiosity.

'He was a good student, they said. He got 412 marks in SSLC, the highest that year in Theeyoor High School. It was in college that he discovered Naxal politics. Soon, he lost interest in his studies and got involved in the Movement. He sold pamphlets at political rallies, attended secret meetings in Kozhikode, even gave public speeches about armed revolution.

'Gopan sir has said to me several times, "Venu was so well-read. It was he who introduced me to Edgar Snow's *Red Star over China*. His death was a great loss for the Movement—a loss in the real sense."

'On the topic of the Naxal Movement, Gopan sir becomes garrulous and emotional. He has endless stories about the risky escapades he had been involved in as part of the Movement, his personal friendships with Varghese and Kisaan Thomman, how he dodged the police when he went to Vellamunda to conduct a study class. According to Jitesh, these are all made-up stories.

'Jitesh had come home once to discuss some party affair with Ravimaman. "How is your principal?" Ravimaman had asked him. "He's not involved with the old Naxals these days, is he?"

"'Even in the old days he barely had any involvement," Jitesh had replied. "He had some vague connection with the attack on Thalassery Police Station. He was a student at Brennen College then. The rest is all a figment of his own imagination—made-up stories of past great deeds to justify to himself that it is okay to make money by running a parallel college and dabbling in real estate."

'Perhaps Jitesh is right. Still, I like Gopan sir for one reason. In making up these stories—even if it is to convince himself that he was a revolutionary—he is making an effort. He recognizes that, to survive this life, we all need a sense of personal significance.'

7.

Conversing with herself had become natural to Krishna, as natural as a daily habit. It had no outward effect on her behaviour or bearing. She had started withdrawing into herself ever since she had finished college and come back to live at home. And when three marriage proposals became unsuccessful in quick succession, she lost all of her innate energy and zest for life. Consciously, she tried to be as unobtrusive as possible, in an effort to efface her very existence within the household. This was when her uncle Ravi took her to Chethana Parallel College and got her a job there. By then, she had become fully introverted, her face a gloomy and unyielding mask that kept people at a distance.

It was only with Shyamedathi and Shantha that the mask came off. In her conversations with Shyamedathi, she was brazen but still maintained certain boundaries. Shantha was the only person she allowed to glimpse her private self. Yet, she had no great secrets to share with Shantha, and the things she did want to talk about were not what Shantha would easily understand. As time went by, Krishna became aware of the possibility that she might never find a companion with whom she could share her intimate thoughts; that she was truly and completely alone. As she became more and more convinced of this possibility, the frequency of her private conversations increased, and she began to feel scared of this habit. She feared that she would lose all control and inadvertently speak out aloud forbidden and dangerous things. Gripped by this fear, she turned to writing. She bought a journal and, under a title instead of a date, in her beautiful handwriting, she wrote out her words as though writing a diary. Sometimes, these took the form of descriptions of events, at other times a soliloquy or a dialogue with an imagined person.

8.

Valliechi is home

Valliechi and the children came in first. Hariyettan paid the taxi driver and followed them carrying a big bag. I watched his slow walk and glum face, and felt uneasy. Valliechi looked glum too, and the children, Amala and Vineesh, gave me a forced smile. I had to wait until last night to find out what was going on.

Hariyettan and Valliechi slept in the room next to mine. Unusually, Amala and Vineesh shared my father's room downstairs. As usual, I woke up with a start at midnight. I heard Valliechi's soft voice from the next room.

'Please tell me what's going on with you.'

'How many times do I have to tell you? There's nothing going on.'

'Then how come you're not interested in me any more?'

'You're imagining things.'

'Who are you kidding? Haven't I known you for the last seventeen years? I've definitely seen a change in the last four months or so.'

'Can't you let me have a peaceful night's sleep, at least when we are here?'

'Why should you sleep when you're the reason I haven't slept in days?'

'How is it my fault?'

'Oh, so nothing is your fault, is it? Look me in the eye and tell me.'

'You think I can't?'

'Well, can you?'

'You've been going on like this for four months!'

'And it's been four months since you started sharing a seat with Lalitha on the train home from work.'

'I give up. I can't fix whatever is wrong with you.'

'Nothing is wrong with me. You're the one who's lost your mind over a tart.'

'Lower your voice. Your sister is in the next room.'

'So what? Let her hear. Let her know what kind of a man the Hariyettan she worships really is.'

The argument continued in that vein for a long time. I think Valliechi wanted me to hear what she was saying. Hariyettan sounded defeated, crestfallen. He didn't sound like a man who had done something wrong, but like someone who once had everything but now had lost all hope.

The uses of television

Amala and Vineesh spend most of the day watching TV. They sit in front of it, silently, as if doing some hard and unpleasant task. They barely talk to Valliechi or Hariyettan. Their cousins, Shanoj and Sarang, have confined themselves to their study room, scared of Vimalechi. So what else could these kids do other than sit in front of the TV?

A dream

I had a horrible dream last night. It started with me jumping out of a window of our house which was on fire. I sprain my foot as I land, and walk away, limping, finally reaching a forest shaped inexplicably like a cave. There's no one else around. Scared and anxious, I walk forward slowly, looking for a way out of there. A little further away, I see Hariyettan. He is dressed like a mendicant and looks exhausted. He tells me, 'This is a terrible place. Further ahead, the trees moulder and form an airless mass with their bent and broken branches all stuck together. Beyond that, there is a high wall. If we can reach it and climb over, we'll be safe.'

It takes us a long time to get to the wall. Along the way, several times, I feel as if I am about to suffocate to death.

Finally, we reach the wall and climb over it. On the other side, we see a dilapidated temple. In the temple yard are hundreds of couples, assembled as if for a communal marriage ceremony. Suddenly, an enormous priest of demonic form appears at the door. He has a gigantic bell in his hand, which he holds above the assembled couples. I cannot remember what happens after that.

In the morning, when I came across Hariyettan at the front of the house, I felt uneasy. Even now, when I think of the dream, I feel a vague sense of guilt.

I didn't go to the meeting

I didn't attend the Women's Association meeting. Shyamedathi came over again to try and persuade me to go. She'd also come because she'd heard Valliechi was home. But Valliechi spoke to her in an offhand manner, as if she couldn't be bothered. She used to look forward to catching up with Shyamedathi, chatting away endlessly with her.

On each of her visits, Valliechi used to remember to bring a gift for Shyamedathi—a handloom sari or sweets from Archana Bakery or a pretty steel vessel, something special like that. Shyamedathi was not the type who yearned for such things, yet she would proudly receive them, saying, 'You shouldn't have, Maya, but I am so happy that you thought of me.'

This time, Valliechi had no gifts for Shyamedathi. She even insinuated that Shyamedathi had only come to see her because she expected to be given something. Shyamedathi flinched when she heard this, her face blanched. 'See you tomorrow at the reading room,' she said to me casually, and left.

This sudden change in Valliechi's attitude must have puzzled Shyamedathi. I guess only Hariyettan knows what is really going on with her. Indeed, there would be no point in any of us trying to figure out what the problem was, because none of us would be able to do anything about it. Valliechi seems to want some fundamental change in Hariyettan, although I wonder if it would help matters. An unbridgeable distance seems to have opened up between them.

Is it true, I wonder, that he was having an affair with this Lalitha whom Valliechi talked about? He is the kind of man women find attractive. Until their last visit, he was handsome and energetic, with a personality to match—well-spoken, dignified. I used to think that Valliechi was blessed to have found someone like him. Oh, how quickly things fall apart! Could all of this be the result of a petty suspicion? Could there be something else going on? I don't think it is right that Valliechi tortures him like this. On this trip, she has been scornful and dismissive, not saying a single loving word to him. Or to her children, for that matter.

Ever since I was a child, the person I have loved most in this household is Valliechi, and she had always returned that love. Her annual trip home was when I felt the happiest and safest. But this time, she has hardly even looked at me properly. I would never have imagined that she would change so completely. Goes to show that we can never be sure of anyone, and that scares me.

Balagopalan

For the first time in years, I ran into Balagopalan. He was doing some fund raising for the annual meeting of a cultural association affiliated to the Congress (I), and had popped in at Chethana to see Gopan sir. He looked hideous in his grey khaddar shirt and dirty mundu, with a scraggly beard and dry hair. The permanent expression of derision on his face added to the overall unpleasantness.

I had gone in to ask Gopan sir about a class schedule when I saw him sitting there, one leg propped up on the other, holding court, flanked by a clutch of young activists. The moment he saw me, he assumed a sense of self-importance.

'Oh, Krishna! So is this where you ended up?' he asked, as though he himself had attained some lofty position in life.

He then turned to Gopan sir and said, 'We were classmates. You know, she is KCR's niece.'

I ignored him completely, talked to Gopan sir, and left.

I've always found Balagopalan repulsive. During pre-degree first year, he was our class representative, and had already assumed the air of a big-time leader. He doesn't seem to have achieved his ambitions even after all these years. Given that the future of the Congress itself is in dire straits, he may never have a chance to fulfil his political ambitions.

People involved in party politics seem to acquire a sense of disdain and derision for everyone else. I see this in Jitesh and Manoj, even in Ravimaman. Do they not go through moments of self-doubt and pain like other ordinary folk? Perhaps not. Or perhaps they are better at shaking those moments off, or if they can't, perhaps they fail as politicians.

Is politics the sum total of individual skills and faults? I should think not. If, as Shyamedathi says, 'this is not what the Party is about,' what exactly is it? Is it about the ideologies and philosophies written in books and newspaper articles? Is a political party anything more than its self-appointed activists?

Politics destroyed Venuvettan's life, while it sustains Ravimaman's. Apart from standing for elections for the post of students' association secretary under the SFI banner, I've had no connection with politics. It plays no part in my current life and has no effect on my job or my friendships. Why, then, am I constantly thinking about it?

Ammini

There is no need for you to know about Ammini. But, since you asked, I will tell you all about her.

Ammini was part of this family long before I was born. My father brought her over from Kunoor. None of us have ever been to Kunoor, although he worked there in the plantations for thirty-eight years. He left my mother in the care of his mother and his unmarried older sister, here in this big house he had inherited and had renovated over the years. It was only after my mother's death that he finally left Kunoor and came back home.

All of us children were born in this house. We were never close to our father, who was home only once every four or five months, each visit bringing with it a certain disquiet and discomfort which only dissipated after he left. He has been home permanently now for over thirteen years—ever since Amma passed away—but he is still a stranger to me.

On one such visit, Achchan brought Ammini home, saying that she would be a help to Amma. Ammini was a child then, barely thirteen years old, and now she is over fifty. In all that time, she's been here with us as though she had no home or family of her own. Ammini is not her real name, but it is the name I have always known her by. She speaks fluent Malayalam, but there still is a trace of Tamil in her accent.

Ammini is dark-skinned, short and stocky and, although she is on the wrong side of fifty, still healthy. In fact, I don't recall a single time when Ammini was unwell.

Ammini is the lightning that struck at the heart of our relationship with Achchan. I was only a child, but I remember a particular day when Amma went to her own house to discuss some property related matters with Ravimaman. She left in the morning and came back in the afternoon. That night, I was woken up from my sleep by Amma's screams and Achchan's loud voice. It was many years later that I understood what the fight had been about: Amma had found out that Ammini had been in their bedroom when she was away, and that Achchan had slept with her.

Throughout my childhood, I feared the days when Achchan was home from Kunoor. Amma was highly strung in his presence, and her distress manifested in violent actions. She beat us silly for no reason at all, broke plates and vessels, and threw away our books, each action aimed at taunting Achchan into a fight. However, she never directed any of her anger or hatred at Ammini, never said a bad word to her. Instead, she turned all her wrath toward Achchan. It was as though she had decided never to give him a moment's peace as punishment for his betrayal. She had always been physically weak, and her feeble body soon developed asthma and eczema and, later, a heart condition.

When Amma died, Ammini was the only one with her. Achchan had gone back to Kunoor a couple of days before. I was in school and my sisters in college.

Amma's death was the fourth in our family. My paternal grandmother died the year I was born. The very next year, on a day with heavy rains, my aunt, Achchan's older sister, went to the river to wash clothes and was swept away in a flash flood. It was two days before they found her body. The next person to die was my brother, Venuvettan. That was really the first time I understood what death was.

My first reaction when Amma died was a sense of relief. In her final days, she had deteriorated so much. Her mind, trapped inside that feeble body, blazed in anger and hatred at anything and everything around her, broiling all of us in its relentless heat.

Ammini, the woman at the heart of all this anguish, continued to live with us after Amma's death. She cooked and cleaned for us, washed our clothes, quietly and without complaint hitched her life to ours, never showing affection or hatred toward any of us, never expecting anything from anyone.

Outside of our family, people talked about Ammini as Achchan's second wife, but we witnessed no sign of the existence of such a relationship between them. Achchan behaved as though he thought of her as little more than a creature that constantly toiled for the family. I have often wondered whether this attitude was something that he developed in his later years.

I don't believe that Amma's suspicions about Ammini and Achchan were entirely unfounded. She was an attractive woman, her beauty the kind that men found sexually appealing and, up until four or five years ago, she had put it to good use. Shantha told me—and I guess I knew this anyway—that she entertained secret paramours in her small room next to the kitchen. Once, when Ravimaman was at home, he heard some noise in the night and came downstairs to investigate. Switching on the light in the hall, he saw someone running from the kitchen and out through the back door. He grabbed a torch and ran after the person, but didn't catch him. The next day, Shantha told me as if it was a secret joke, 'Hey, you know Vasu, the plasterer? He fell down the quarry last night and broke his arm and leg. They've taken him to the Medical College Hospital, so he'll live, I guess.'

That evening, when I went into the kitchen for my coffee, I saw Ammini sobbing quietly and wiping her eyes.

Valliechi and Hariyettan have gone

Valliechi and Hariyettan went back on the afternoon train. They'd been arguing all day yesterday, their voices louder than usual. I lay in my bed listening to them until, at some point, I fell asleep.

It was only when I saw Amala ironing her churidar that I knew they were leaving. Fresh from her shower and decked out in a sandalwood-coloured silk sari and jewellery, Valliechi showed no sign of the previous night's argument. Amazing! Valliechi had never been one for fancy clothes or jewellery, always content in her voile saris and never pestering Hariyettan for necklaces or bangles. What an extraordinary transformation in just one year!

I am amazed at Vimalechi too. She was bound to have known that things were not all right between Valliechi and Hariyettan, but she didn't seem the least bit concerned. If anything, she seemed more upbeat than usual, laughing and chatting even when Valliechi remained morose, narrating in great detail Shanoj winning first prize for poetry writing at the school talent day and Sarang acing his exams. Listening to her go on and on, I felt irritated.

Dasettan has also been behaving strangely. Until last year, he treated Hariyettan with deference, but this time around he acted as though he hadn't even noticed that Hariyettan was home. He pretended to be too busy to talk to him, leaving home right after breakfast and not returning until the evening. And when he finally came home, it was with his friends—

Kunnumbrath Unnikrishnan or someone else of his ilk. He then pulled up some chairs under the mango tree and sat chatting with them, completely ignoring Hariyettan. I don't even recognize many of his new friends. I ran into one of them this morning at the bus stop, a scary looking fellow with a vertical slash of vermillion on his forehead.

As they were leaving, Hariyettan and the children looked crestfallen. Ravimaman had taken some time off his busy schedule and come home to see them off, and he looked glum as well. My father's expression was, as usual, difficult to read, as he watched them leave. Valliechi ignored the whole lot of us, and walked away as if she had not a care in the world. Silently saying goodbye to us, Hariyettan and the children followed. My heart breaks even now, thinking about that scene.

Home / Prison

It's been a week since Valliechi left. Somehow it seems longer.

Whenever they visited, I used to take Amala and Vineesh to the temple and to the riverside. They are beautiful children, both in their looks and in their behaviour, and I used to feel proud taking them around. This time, though, they didn't come into my room even once. Scared and distrustful of everyone, they withdrew into themselves.

Since Valliechi left, Vimalechi's behaviour toward me has become worse. If she finds me at the front of the house, she looks daggers at me and asks, 'What are you doing, standing here?' I have to field a hundred questions from her if I'm a little late coming back from work. She monitors my every move until I go upstairs to my room after dinner.

What happened today has convinced me that there is

something seriously wrong with her. I'd washed my clothes in the morning and hung them up to dry on the clothesline. A little later, as I looked out of my window, I saw Vimalechi approach the clothesline and, glancing around to make sure no one was watching, she threw her dirty underskirt over my bra and panties.

At tea, she asked me, out of the blue, 'Did you go to Dasettan's school, day before yesterday?'

'No.'

'Then who was it that went to see him?'

'How would I know?'

She glared at me, as if she didn't believe me.

Every moment that I am out of my room, she watches me like a hawk. I have to watch my every move, and be extra careful to avoid being in the presence of Dasettan.

Dasettan, meanwhile, is barely home these days, and even when he is around, I don't have to be too scared of him. The association with Unnikrishnan and the others seems to have changed him somehow; their new politics seems to have gone to his head. He didn't come home last night, and didn't seem to have bothered telling Vimalechi. 'Did he tell you anything?' she asked me—twice. I felt sorry for her. How did she get to a point where she imagines that he'd tell me things that he wouldn't tell his wife?

There's something wrong with every single person in this house. Achchan lives here as if he is all alone. Well, he's got only himself to blame for that. Amma spent a large part of her life in a red haze of anger. Venuvettan went away pursuing a dream and ended up nowhere. Vimalechi—and now Valliechi too—seems set to follow in Amma's footsteps. Achchan's fate awaits Hariyettan and Dasettan. All of them caught in a single mistake: they got married and became husbands and wives. The only normal people in this house are Ammini and I. In fact, Ammini is better off than I am—I don't have her mental strength, her resilience.

Vimalechi didn't sleep a wink last night. This was the first time Dasettan had stayed away from home overnight, leaving her to imagine what horrible scenarios, I don't know. I've been entertaining my own horrible thoughts—that he spent the night with Lillykutty teacher in some hotel room. I have been having many bad thoughts in the last couple of days. I say 'bad' only because those are the kind of thoughts that people generally consider bad. If you think about it that way, wouldn't everyone who is married be bad?

I indulge in the 'bad' in secret, on my own, letting myself overflow and be drenched. It is like unseen seeds sprouting in a narrow valley, growing with abandon and filling it with soft, luscious greenery. I imagine a strong arm holding my body and ringing it like a small bell. It is an exquisite sensation, its weight heavy on my closing eyelids, and I lose myself in it.

In the morning, as I lay awake in my bed gripped by lethargy, I heard Dasettan's voice shouting, 'This is not a prison, is it? I'll go wherever I want, whenever I please.'

Eventually, I got to know from Manoj where Dasettan had been that night. The Marxist Party activists set fire to BJP flags and posters in Chenkara. Dasettan had gone to speak at the protest meeting organized by the BJP. 'You should have heard his speech,' Manoj said. 'When did he learn all this Sanskrit? His speech was peppered with quotations from the Bhagavad Gita.'

I am as surprised as Manoj. When did Dasettan begin reading the Gita? Where, indeed, did he learn Sanskrit?

History

I lost my temper with Reshma, and I am glad. She needed to be taken down a peg or two. Such arrogance! How dare she criticize my Indian history class notes in front of the pre-degree first year B-batch students? A degree and a BEd in history do not make a person a history pundit.

What really pissed me off was Asha's interference in our discussion. She thinks she knows everything. The ability to speak English fluently does not make you an authority on everything in the world. What is her qualification? That she lived and studied in Bombay? And then what happened? Look at where she is now! Her parents got divorced, and now she and her mother live here, on their own. The way she dresses and carries on, you'd think she's just stepped out of a palace. Well, if she was so well-off, she wouldn't come to work in a parallel college, would she? It's all very well to be perfectly turned out, but what about her attitude? No wonder Gopan sir hesitates to appoint female staff. In fact, there are only the three of us in Chethana, while there are nineteen male teachers. 'Lady teachers will find it difficult to manage a class of over eighty students,' Gopan sir says. I know the real reason he doesn't want to appoint women is that women can't get along with each other unless they have a great deal of social sense, and that's not guaranteed just because one knows some English.

'History is a serious subject,' she told me, as if I need her to tell me that. Besides, how much serious teaching do the students here need? All they want is pre-written notes. Or some guide books which they can easily buy for twenty or twenty-five rupees. And if they read them, they will easily get a first class result. They don't even need to know the first thing about what constitutes history. There was a really good sentence about history in *The God of Small Things*. I should have written it down, it was that brilliant. But I'd borrowed the book from Harish who insisted I return it in two days, so I didn't get the chance. Shame I can't afford my own copy—where would I find an extra 395 rupees?

He won't come

I am a fool.

I indulged in so many fantasies about Dileepan—that he'd come back, that my life would change because of him . . .

At times, loneliness is a terrible feeling. I feel that I am all alone at the edge of an infinite, deserted valley. And in those moments, my thoughts go to him; my body presses on to his, melting into it like wax.

I know these thoughts, these imagined wonders, are pointless. He won't come.

Dileepan must be wandering through some other forests now, searching for other plants. I'm here still, alone in this room. His memories grow around me like green shoots, tangled vines and majestic trees, and I am overwhelmed by a peculiar desire. I want to be not me. I want to shed this female body and human existence. Instead, I want to transform into a dense forest, and I want him to know me, walk through me, touching and smelling, plucking out whatever it is that he is looking for.

Shantha is dead

Suicide. For you, it is material for a news story. Especially when there have been four suicides in the same village within a month, and the last death is suspected to be a murder.

So I was not surprised to see you among the crowd that had gathered in Shantha's front yard. You'd come for the details—the story of her death and that of the others. Why were the young people in this village gripped by depression? Why did some of them, with seemingly no major problems in life, kill themselves? I'm sure people would have given you many answers—breakdown in values, the competitiveness that consumes life itself, the innate fragility of the nuclear family, alcoholism, sexual permissiveness—and I am sure you'd address each of them carefully in your report. You're focused on the recognition such a considered report will bring you. There's nothing wrong with that. Just as history and the poems and stories in the pre-degree textbooks serve me a purpose, the suicides, power politics and accidents serve you.

I don't know why Shantha killed herself or, indeed, was murdered. She hadn't come to see me in a while. She is smart and would have noticed that Vimalechi was not happy about her coming to our house. She would have stayed away to avoid causing more trouble for me.

I ran into her yesterday in front of Hotel Chandradas, opposite the bus stop outside Chethana. She was with two men I'd never seen before. I assumed one was the contractor she used to talk about. The other man was fair-skinned, dressed in a shirt and trousers, with a pair of sunglasses on his clean-shaven, fleshy face. He had an out-of-state look. I said to myself that there was something dodgy about him. The bus stop was crowded with students from Chethana, and she may not have seen me. Now I can't help but wonder whether she was pretending not to have seen me.

It was Divakaran who told us the news when he delivered milk this morning, that Shantha's body had been discovered hanging from a cashew nut tree in her yard. Divakaran enjoys delivering such salacious news along with the milk. He described how her feet were touching the ground and how there was a wound on her forehead. 'She didn't kill herself,' he added. 'Someone definitely killed her and hung her up. Any idiot could see that.'

You'd be surprised to know that I wasn't shocked by the news, that I didn't feel even a pang of sorrow.

I was surprised, though, that when I set out to her house, Vimalechi came with me. She didn't say anything, just followed me silently.

As you know, it was noon by the time they brought her body home after the post mortem. I didn't go inside to look at it. Not because I couldn't face it, but because I didn't want to see Shantha like that. Vimalechi went in and, when she came out, her eyes were red. 'Come, let's leave,' she said and hurried out of there. She seemed more anxious than sad, and I'm not quite sure why.

It's late in the night now. My head hurts from the harsh light of this table lamp. Why am I still awake? Shantha's death has still not sunk in. It's just that, since morning, something like a fog seems to have enveloped my mind, and I find myself unable to recall any memories of her.

The scent of peppercorns

A long time ago, there was a small patch of woods behind Theeyoor Lower Primary School. Just a cluster of trees, really – a soapnut tree, an ezhilam pala, a couple of coral trees, and some other nameless wild trees and bushes. We used to play there sometimes and, occasionally, a rabbit or a mongoose would come out of the bushes to entertain us. I remember seeing a big black rat snake there once.

It was in those woods that I first experienced the scent of ripe peppercorns.

On that day, Shantha and I had reached the school quite early.

'Do you want to see something?' Shantha asked me, as if there was something special and precious she wanted to share.

'What is it?' I was curious.

'Come,' she said, and together we climbed over the fence and went into the woods.

We sat with our legs stretched out on the flat rock under the ezhilam pala. She put her hand inside the pocket of her dress and pulled out the thing that was supposed to amaze me: a handful of ripe red peppercorns! Most of them had bruised and burst.

'Is this the big deal?' I was not impressed.

'Eat some,' Shantha said. 'They're delicious. You have to spit out the seeds. Otherwise it will be too spicy,' she reminded me.

Shantha and I ate those peppercorns one by one, savouring their mild sweetness and intoxicating fragrance. When we finished, Shantha licked her lips with the tip of her tongue and said, 'Now look. What do you think?'

Her lips were tinged red and she looked beautiful.

'So red,' I said.

'So are yours, Krishna,' she said. 'You look so pretty.'

I stood up and, giving into some impulse that suddenly welled up inside me, pressed my lips against hers. The scent of ripe peppercorns enveloped us in its sweet wonderment.

An assault on Dasettan

Last night, Dasettan was assaulted by a group of Marxist activists in front of the telephone booth in Theeyoor market. They accused him of behaving inappropriately with the young woman who ran the telephone booth. The BJP is arguing that he has been wrongly accused, and that the assault was politically driven. The local newspapers have covered the story in great detail, including pictures of him on his hospital bed and a statement from the BJP district secretary.

Divakaran says that Dasettan was alone when he was set upon by a group of seven or eight people. He's lost a tooth and has sustained injuries to his legs, back and forehead.

Some people came in a jeep to take Vimalechi and Achchan to the hospital. Achchan went with them, but Vimalechi refused to go. 'I don't care what happens to him,' she seemed to say. The children, Shanoj and Sarang, wanted to go, but one scary look from Vimalechi and they went back into their room. It was that same look that stopped me in my tracks too, but now I feel that I shouldn't have allowed myself to be intimidated. If nothing else, Dasettan was a member of this family, and we should all have gone to the hospital at least as a matter of courtesy.

There'd be no one to stay at the hospital to take care of him.

Ever since he married Vimalechi, he has been estranged from his own family.

Dasettan's family was old money. They were known as the 'Singapore folk'. His father had been a businessman in Singapore for many years, and after he retired he set up a business in Theeyoor. It turned out to be a failure. They get by because all the children are settled relatively well, but they pretend to be better than everyone else. The mother is the worst. After her wedding, Vimalechi stayed with them only for three days because she had a huge argument with the woman. She sat up an entire night hurling abuses at Vimalechi and our entire family. The next morning, Vimalechi came back home crying and carrying on, and before noon Dasettan came to join her. And that was that. Neither of them has visited his family since then.

Dasettan had always been somewhat pompous and lazy, and everyone was surprised when Vimalechi fell in love with him and decided to marry him.

Dasettan is not cut out to be a political activist. When he was in college, he used to hang out with some KSU activists, which led to some involvement in the Congress Party. All he did was entertain the party leaders and go around with them. He squandered a lot of money doing that, which caused some serious problems between him and Vimalechi. He seems to have no particular skills other than flirting with women. If he did, and given how close he was to the powers that be, he'd have been a big shot within the party by now.

There seems to be some big secret behind his recent defection from the Congress to the BJP. Joining the BJP is not the same as being involved with the Congress—it is a dangerous thing to do. Ever since my school days, there's been a bitter rivalry between the local BJP and the Marxists. Last year, there was a pitched battle just at the corner of our road, which ended in one man's death.

Ordinarily, Dasettan is not the kind of person to get involved in anything that would be dangerous. Nor is his change of track the result of some ideological differences. I wonder if he decided to be self-destructive because he had anyway lost his peace of mind. I wonder if the constant expression of tiredness and dejection on his face is a sign of having given up. If that is the case, I can't help but feel a bit sorry for him. If nothing else, he left his own family to be with Vimalechi, didn't he? And now . . .

Demonstrations

By the time I left work and got to the market, the whole place was in chaos. Activists from the BJP and the Marxist Party faced off against each other, shouting slogans at the top of their voices. The two groups of demonstrators were separated by a battalion of police. All the shops were closed and people hurried away in all directions. My legs were heavy with fear as I, too, hurried home.

I'm not sure when the demonstrators left. A while ago on the road below, there was a torchlight procession by the Marxist Party, swiftly followed by the BJP. Last year, on a day with similar demonstrations, the groups threw hand grenades at each other at the corner. I wonder what calamity we are in for this year.

Joseph's wife

I have a special piece of news today: I met Joseph's wife.

After lunch, I took a short break from Chethana, hoping to

pop in to the exhibition of Surat saris at the Hotel Ashoka near the Telephone Bhavan. Reshma had bought a sari at the sale there, and I wanted to have a look.

I turned on to Post Office Road hoping to avoid the crowds and ran straight into Joseph. A blue Maruti was parked at the kerb and a woman was huddled next to it. The man with her was facing away from me, but I recognized him instantly.

I was about to turn around and walk away when he saw me.

'Hey, Krishna!' He didn't try to hide his surprised happiness at running into me. Joseph's wife stood up and wiped her mouth with a handkerchief.

'This is Krishna, my classmate,' Joseph introduced me to her. He patted his wife's shoulder and told me, 'You know who this is—Clara.'

Clara smiled. I searched frantically for something nice to say but, before I could say anything, Joseph continued, 'We're on our way back from visiting her brother in Kannur. She's been feeling nauseous since the Chavakkad Gate.'

Joseph's wife gave me another pale smile.

'We must get on,' Joseph said, his hand on the front door of the car. They got in and drove away.

I didn't go to Ashoka after all, suddenly feeling out of sorts.

Joseph's wife was quite beautiful. She was pregnant, but her face was that of an innocent young girl. You could tell she was from a well-to-do family by the way she was dressed, in a posh salwar-kameez. Not very tall though. Even in her high heels, she barely came up to Joseph's chest.

I am amazed at how unfazed Joseph seemed running into me like that, how casually he introduced me to his wife. Had we been there a while longer, I feel he'd probably have told her all about how close we were. Of course, it could all have been an act, because he did seem somewhat eager to get away. Otherwise, why would he not have asked me how I was doing? After all, it has been a long time since we'd seen each other.

To be honest, I started sweating profusely from the moment I saw him. Running into him like that, what I felt was not sadness but a sense of embarrassment. I can't explain it. And in the evening, on my way back home, something else happened. The bus was about to leave JS Corner when a young man came running and jumped into it. He was perhaps around eighteen, but was quite well-built. An ordinary looking guy. I had seen him before in the bus. Once he'd sat in the seat behind me and started some fun and games, rubbing his knees against my back. I'd turned around and said loudly, 'What?' After which he sat looking out of the window with an innocent expression.

Today, the bus was packed. Not an inch of space was left as it moved away from JS Corner. I watched him squeeze himself through the crowd to the front of the bus. I was laughing inside. He came up behind me, and stood with his body pressed against mine. And how! Well, let him, I thought, and didn't move away.

A while later, the conductor came along. 'Move over there,' he said to the young man.

'Where? Where's the space?'

'Space? I'll get your old man to come and make some space,' said the conductor aggressively, and pushed him.

And that was it. People started pushing and shouting, 'Move over, you scoundrel.' 'Don't let him get away.' 'Push the bastard out.'

The driver stopped the bus. The young man jumped out

and ran away, and the crowd erupted, laughing and whistling and, until the bus pulled into the market, everyone joined in making fun of the young man and calling him names.

I laughed right along with them although, inside, I felt a pang of guilt. After all, I had encouraged him, albeit tacitly, to stand the way he did, pressing against me.

Dineshan has been murdered

Shyamedathi's son, Dineshan, was hacked to death by a bunch of RSS supporters. Apparently, they went to the soda factory where he worked, dragged him out and, in broad daylight, cut off both his legs and then finished him off with a hatchet.

In the past, Theeyoor had lost people to bombings and knife attacks. But these acts had always been done under the cover of darkness. Never has there been a murder as brazen as this, in plain view in the middle of the market.

Dineshan took part in demonstrations by DYFI and the Marxist Party from time to time, but he had never been in trouble before. After the demolition of Babri Masjid, the Red Star Arts and Sports Club in Thiyoor had staged a one-act play in protest. Dineshan had been involved in that. Apart from that, he'd always stayed away from party-based altercations. In fact, he was not brave or strong enough to get himself involved.

His murderers, a group of five or six people, had come in a jeep. One of them was a guy from Chenkara who was also the main accused in last year's bombing. The rest were from out of town.

His hacked-up body lay there for about ten minutes before anyone would approach it. People were frozen in terror.

Dineshan was Shyamedathi's only child. I cannot even

begin to imagine the agony she must be going through. My heart breaks, thinking of her lying in the corner of her veranda like a bundle of old clothes, too shocked to even cry.

Dineshan's murder has stunned the entire town. After the funeral, there was a meeting in front of Shyamedathi's house. Ravimaman spoke at the meeting, but he could barely get two or three sentences out before he broke down. I could not bear to see it and had to turn away and cover my face. Every single person there was crying.

Terror

I am stuck in an ancient cave reeking of unidentified dangers. I am all alone. There is only one word to describe what I am feeling: terror.

I've heard so much about Dineshan's murder since yesterday—about his hacked-off limbs, the animal screams of his dying agony, the terrifying silence of his killers.

Last night, even before it was dark, Achchan locked all the doors and switched on all the lights. He's done it again tonight.

I was at Chethana when I heard the news. 'Leave quickly,' Gopan sir told us. 'There'll be no buses today.'

I left with twenty or so students who were from my town. In the blazing sun, we walked the six kilometres into town and, by the time we were walking down the hill toward the market, we'd become part of a large crowd.

I haven't left the house today. I thought of going to see Shyamedathi, but couldn't muster up the courage.

In the evening, Divakaran came to tell us that there would be no milk delivery in the morning. I overheard him talking to my father about Shyamedathi. They took her to the hospital last

night, he said, and she is still slipping in and out of consciousness. His poor father seems to have lost his mind. He behaves
as if he doesn't know that his son has been killed, laughing and
chatting with everyone and inviting them to tea.

'They know who the killers are,' Divakaran said. 'None of
them will be alive for more than a month. Do you think the
Marxists will sit back and do nothing?'

No, they won't. Neither will their opponents. There will be
no peace of mind in this place for a very long time.

I had an early dinner which I barely ate, and shut myself in
this room. I have been lying here ever since with the door and
windows locked. All that my mind can come up with are scary
thoughts about the future.

Dasettan is still in the hospital. It seems that he has sustained a serious injury to his spine. Some people say that
Dineshan's murder was retribution for the attack on Dasettan.
The local RSS activists, including Kunnumbrath Unnikrishnan,
are in hiding. I fear that the Marxists might attack our house,
frustrated that they can't get to the others.

Ravimaman usually doesn't spend the night here, unless he
gets back into town late after a long journey. If he decides to
stay over one of these days, the RSS lot would definitely hear
about it. They too would be watching.

Apart from Achchan and Vimalechi's two boys, it's just us
three women here. But that won't stop those who come determined to cause harm. Anyone is fair game for those who have
decided on killing and maiming. A few years ago, they killed a
boy at the bus terminus. He was only sixteen years old. He was
on his way back from collecting his school-leaving certificate.
A case of mistaken identity, they said. To date, nobody knows
who the culprits are.

All day, I have been thinking up such scary thoughts. And I am not the only one who's scared. I can see fear in Achchan and Ammini. Ammini, especially, seems to have lost her fortitude and looks shaken. The person I find amazing—and disgusting—is Vimalechi. In the midst of all this worry, I saw her sitting Shanoj and Sarang down and making them do their homework. What is the point in that, in this forced education, when they are not even given the freedom to be scared? What will they learn? What type of human beings will they be when they grow up? Education be damned. Lack of education has never been the main problem with this world.

Shantha's visit

Yesterday, Shantha came to see me during my daytime nap. She was dressed in a light violet blouse with small puff sleeves and a violet sari printed with big flowers.

There was only one difference between this Shantha and the Shantha who had been alive. She spoke in a language that I could not understand. It had a beautiful rhythm, and words as light as butterflies. She looked happier and more beautiful than ever.

Anti-social elements

The newspapers report that Theeyoor is regaining normalcy, the journalists suggesting that the people have returned to their familiar ruts, pushing the fallout from Dineshan's murder into the recesses of their collective memory. After all, how long can the destruction of crops and property, the burning and the stoning be sustained? How long can the youth on both sides of the political divide live in hiding? The District Collector had presided over a peace meeting and requested the public to isolate the anti-social elements bent upon causing trouble.

Who, exactly, are these anti-social elements? If they are a specific group, how are they formed? Who sustains them?

Today, for the first time in a week, I ventured out of the house. The faces of the people I met along the way and in the market were frozen and dark with the shadow of fear and anxiety.

On my way back from Chethana, I ran into Ambujam's father, Narayanan Nair. He had a stroke almost a year ago, and watching his slow limping gait as he leaned on his walking stick, I felt sorry for him.

Ambujam and I were roommates in college. She'd moved to Bombay after her marriage eight years ago. I'd seen her only two or three times since then.

Narayanan Nair has a nickname—Aani Nair. A name he'd acquired because of his propensity to insert himself into people's affairs like a nail and cause harm. In the days of the revolt, he's said to have been a police informant, spying on the Communists. Later, he began to inform on Communists who worked in the army and other central government offices. He's been responsible for many of them, including Ravimaman, losing their jobs. Despite a lifetime of troublemaking, he's survived until the ripe old age of seventy-five without much harm to himself.

As soon as he saw me, he stopped, leaned on his walking stick, and said, 'How are you, child?'

'Good.'

'No prospects of marriage yet, eh?'

'No.'

'Ah, what to do . . . ? Each according to her destiny. We

desire one thing, but the gods decide something else for us,' he said, as if empathizing with me, and laughed.

I was embarrassed. Without bothering to reply, I hurried away. Unfortunately, the next person I met was worse than Aani Nair. Dakshayani Amma, the woman who looked after Dr Gangadharan's children. She came down the lane, turned on to the road and, catching sight of me, paused and fell in step with me.

'Your Dasettan is not out of the hospital yet, is he?'

'Not yet.'

I was convinced that there was a hidden meaning in her usage of the word 'your'. I didn't let on that I had noticed.

'Vimala didn't go to the hospital to see him, did she?'

'No.'

'Did you?'

'I haven't either.'

'Oh. Why ever not! He may have fallen out with your sister, but he still likes you, doesn't he?' she said, laughing. She winked at me and pooched out her lips.

I lost my temper. 'Have you got nothing else to do other than keeping track of people's likes and dislikes?' I shouted. 'Getting on a bit, aren't you? Time to stop this silly gossip-mongering.'

Without waiting for a response, I walked quickly away from her.

Moonlight and silence

A moonlit night. As I sit here watching the night, I realize that moonlight is also silence. The neem, mango and guava trees in the yard stand perfectly still, as though lost within themselves.

It's been a long time since I have watched moonlight. And not just moonlight, I have also stopped looking at flowers or birds. All of it, nature itself, seems to have disappeared from my life.

I have listened to many speakers argue that we humans have become alienated from nature because of our busy, competitive lifestyles. I don't think that's a factor in my life.

Yes, I go to work every day, but I don't have a busy schedule. Nor am I in competition with anyone. I go to Chethana, teach, come back and spend the rest of the time here in this room. I could go downstairs, but I have nothing to share with anyone. I could pass the time sitting in front of the TV, but Vimalechi doesn't like to have the TV on. She says it distracts the children from their studies. In any case, I have no particular interest in watching TV.

The only enjoyable thing to do, sitting here in this room, is reading. I subscribe to two magazines and check out books and journals from the library at Chethana, and occasionally borrow newly published fiction from Harish or Jitesh. Reading is the one habit of mine that has endured over the years. I feel out of sorts if I don't spend at least some of my time reading. Lately, though, even this habit has begun to feel boring and pointless. What I read now makes me feel like being pushed down a street full of mechanical dolls moving their lips.

Much of contemporary writing feels insipid to me, and reading it feels like hard work. The writers don't seem to be emotionally invested in their own words or have a sense of commitment to what they write about. When I read a book, I want to feel that the writer is extending his or her fingers and touching my skin. Without that feeling, I disconnect. The only books that have touched me like that recently, made me feel ener-gized, are Marquez's *Love in the Time of Cholera* and Arundhati Roy's *The God of Small Things*. Even then, I was bored by the time I got to the end of Marquez's novel. I think he overdid the character of Florentino Ariza. That business with the schoolgirl was truly appalling and unnecessary.

Not finding anything interesting to read is a kind of tor-ture. I don't have to do much preparation for my classes. I have plenty of class notes for history, prepared using a couple of guidebooks and textbooks. I just have to talk for a bit and then give them the notes. As for teaching the Malayalam classes, I have a couple of guidebooks for that too. Everything else can be sorted out by flicking through the *Sabdatharavali* and the dic-tionary of the Puranas.

'After all, what's there to teach in the humanities?' John from Commerce had declared one day to get a rise out of Jitesh, and started a heated discussion in the staffroom. He is partly right. Who needs history or literature these days? People just want to get by, and all they are interested in are things that make their lives comfortable. Especially the new generation. They don't let themselves be worried about complex matters. They dabble in politics and arts, but never to the extent that it penetrates their skins. They are not affected by what happens around them. And they have no interest in learning anything new from life or from books. All they want is their class notes, and if you can retain a sense of humour while delivering them, they remain interested. My colleagues have all become adept at this. There's constant laughter in Jitesh's and Manoj's classrooms. Reshma is not bad either in telling jokes and horsing around. As for me, I become completely serious once I enter the classrooms.

To be honest, I am not cut out to be a teacher. I think I'd like a different kind of life, but I can't quite describe what kind of life that would be. But I am sure of one thing—no matter how much I crave for a different kind of life, I am never going to achieve it.

Sajini's wedding

Sajini from next door is getting married today. The racket of the celebration began yesterday. I could hear the sound of the electric generator late into the night. The lane leading to her house has been decorated with colourful bulbs, tube lights and shining arches.

Our families have never got on well with each other. Still, Sajini's parents came to invite us to the wedding. Achchan popped in for a little while last evening, just to be polite. He hasn't said anything to Vimalechi or me about attending the wedding. It has been a long time since either of us went to a wedding.

From my window, I can see into their front yard. At least five hundred people must have visited them yesterday. They are not that well off, so I don't know how they managed to invite so many people and feed them all biriyani. And today, two busloads of people came. Sajini's father is a shop assistant in a grocery store, and one of her brothers is a lorry driver. Without other sources of income in the family, I wonder how they managed to put up such a spectacle.

But this is a miracle that happens all around us these days. Even those who don't have a steady source of income seem to be able to take care of their affairs properly—buy big houses, dress smartly, and live with no apparent anxieties. It's when I notice this that I feel a sense of inferiority and hatred for my family. Why were we the only ones failing to make something of ourselves?

The tribal

Chethana was like a bereaved house this afternoon. A student of second-year economics, Shirley, was arrested with two of her male classmates at a hotel on the beach. Gopan sir has managed to deal with the matter without much damage, but the news of the arrest has spread among the people.

Last year, Shirley had performed a dance for the College Day. The compere had mistakenly announced it as 'tribal dance' instead of folk dance and, since then, everyone had started calling her 'the tribal'.

Shirley had come onstage dressed in a skimpy black silk cloth tied low around her waist and a tight black blouse. And for the next five to eight minutes, she had 'performed' something—biting her lips, giving come-hither looks, jerking her waist, and turning this way and that . . . The applause and wolf whistles from the students were deafening. The whole thing came to a climax when she kneeled down on the stage and gyrated in a circle.

Next day, there was a staff meeting in which a decision was made to screen future College Day performances beforehand. Gopan sir had called Shirley in and admonished her. But she had not been bothered at all, and continued with her come-hither looks and condescending smiles as she stomped around the college.

It seems that this was not the first time Shirley had been found using that hotel. Apparently, she was once caught with 'an uncle' in this same hotel. Who knows what other stories we'll hear about her? I'm sure there will be more in the newspapers. Good—at least there will be something interesting to read.

In the bus

I've had a dull ache in my lower abdomen since morning. I have it occasionally. The effect is more like mental fatigue than physical pain—as if something dark broods within me.

I considered not going to Chethana today, but the thought of spending all day at home made me change my mind.

I caught the 9.45 'Jawahar' bus. The cleaner grabbed me by my arse and pushed me into the bus through the milling bodies of men standing on the footboard. I was mortified.

The bus was so crowded that there was barely space for a needle. Men and women stuck together without space to even breathe. I was prodded and squeezed and jostled about. People muttered in hatred and frustration.

It is when you travel in a crowded bus that you fully understand human nature. No one has a kind word to say, and everyone seems to look for an opportunity to treat others with indignity. Oh, I suffered the full horror of it today.

9.

'This writing is useless. After all, I'm not even a writer,' Krishna held up her pen and said to herself one night. 'I did something silly ten or eleven years ago. Jayamohan had been the college magazine editor then. One day, he came up to me and asked, "Krishna, could you submit a short story for the magazine?"

'"Me? A short story?"

'"Why the look of surprise? I know just by looking at you that you are a writer."

'"Go away. Stop pulling my leg."

'"Pulling your leg? Me? Why would you think that, Krishna?"

'Jayamohan was a shameless flirt in those days, and women seemed to enjoy his flirtations. That's why he won the election by three hundred votes, while all the other SFI candidates lost.

'Although Jayamohan's request was just another attempt to flirt with me, I decided to take it seriously, and one afternoon I sat in my room and wrote a story inside of an hour. "Blue Lagoons"—that was the title of the story, but I can't quite recall what it was about. Anyway, when I gave it to Jayamohan, it was his turn to be surprised. He published it in the magazine, and I got a lot of compliments from people. Still, I never wrote another story. If I had focused on that aspect of my life, I might perhaps have become a famous writer. Too late now. I can't even think about writing, except for these jottings just for my own pleasure. This is a pointless exercise. No one finds it useful.'

Then Krishna had a fearful thought: What if she died suddenly one night, and Vimalechi or someone else found her notes and read them? She put her pen down and sat quietly, as though engulfed in a mist. She didn't write anything that night. The night after that, when she sat down to write, she was gripped by the same fearful thought. So she abandoned her habit of writing in her journal. For the next four or five nights, she sat in her room, suffocating without an outlet for her thoughts and, when she could stand it no more, she resumed her habit of talking to herself.

10.

'Gopan sir, you should not have done this to me. I was very uncomfortable when you sent Varghese to fetch me from my classroom, saying that you wanted to introduce me to this man who was supposed to be an old friend of my brother. I know some of your old friends from your extremist politics days come to visit you every now and then. "The armed revolutionaries financed by Gopan sir"—Jitesh jokes about them. I thought, at first, that this man might be one of those. But when you introduced us and left the room leaving us alone, I was really uncomfortable.

'He said he was an art critic and lived in Madras. The way he spoke Malayalam with that accent—it irritated me. What was he, a foreigner? And how much he talked in a matter of minutes—sexual freedom, vulgar morality, mutual understanding, ideology . . . At the end of it all, in his slithery language, a proposal for marriage.

'Ravimaman hasn't entrusted you with the job of finding me a husband, has he? I haven't asked for your help either. So what right do you have to interfere? You may be under some illusions, but I know exactly what these men are like.

'He must have been at least fifteen years older than me. Let's overlook the age difference for a minute, but what about those tobacco-stained teeth in that flabby mouth, and that mouldy old shirt? Oh . . . Let's disregard that too, but that self-proclaimed attitude of being a great scholar—that really is something.

'I may not have the right or eligibility to judge other people, but let me tell you something: that man was a complete moron.'

11.

'I read the first instalment of "A Village Burning in Agony". I like the title you've given to the series. In fact, I can't imagine a better title for a story about this village.

'Like Nooranad and Kayaralam, Theeyoor is also turning into a "suicide village". You've made some good general observations about this place. The statistics about suicides in the state, the demographic breakdown of deaths by suicide and methods of suicides—all of these have made the article a piece of serious scholarship. Jayamohan, I think this series will get you noticed as a journalist to be reckoned with. So here's some information about one more suicide for the last part of your series: Divakaran, the man who used to deliver our milk, killed himself this morning by drinking brandy mixed with pesticide.

'Divakaran killed himself because he was drowning in debt. He was one of those people sent to this earth only to live a life of penury and misery. He had a large family to look after—a wife and two children, a father who was ill, a mentally disabled sister, several other relatives dependent on him. Divakaran had no proper work. He got on by delivering milk from the cooperative society to a few houses, and running errands for people—paying their electricity bills, getting their groceries from the ration shop, and so on. His health allowed him to do only such odd-jobs, and he'd managed so far. Whenever things got dire, he'd borrow some money from someone. He'd borrowed money even from me—a couple of hundred rupees. He'd never been able to pay them back.

'Last month, his child was hospitalized because of dysentery. And then it was his wife's sister's wedding. He must have suffocated, caught between all these demands.

'His death was no surprise to anyone. What else could he do—people seem to be asking. Even I felt the same. If this is all we can think or feel when a human life is lost, it should scare us all. Is there any meaning in being alive if this is the best we can do?'

12.

'These days, I have nobody to share my personal life with. Shantha is dead. Dileepan is far away, both physically and mentally. As for Jayamohan, what significance would the personal life of someone like me have in his world? He is only interested in newsworthy stories. And Joseph, well, he is another woman's husband, and I have no right to share my private life with him. These are the facts. No amount of wishful thinking on my part will change them. And, really, there is no point in me talking to any of them, even if it is only in my imagination. But what can I do? I have to talk to someone until I fall asleep. Otherwise, I would feel like running out of the house, even if it is the middle of the night. I cannot knowingly fling myself into a situation where everyone would think that I've lost all mental control and gone mad.

'That's why, Reshma, I've decided to talk with you today, tell you all about what happened in my life on this one day. You know we don't have a relationship that allows for such intimate conversations. We exchange a couple of words because we are colleagues, and I know that you don't expect a friendship that goes beyond that from me. You have a prickly character that suits your thin, dry body. The only time it changes is when you are in the classroom—you are very good at entertaining the students, and being a teacher is the job best suited for you. But your instinct to put others down so that you can feel superior is something you should try and curb. Could you not stop your habit of causing trouble for others and then pretending that you had nothing to do with it?

'If you think about it, there are very few reasons for us to be unfriendly to each other. In fact, there are more reasons that should have encouraged a friendship between us. We are both unmarried. Given your looks and family circumstances, you are as unlikely to get married as me. So we share a disappointment. And there's bound to be other disappointments that we share that we don't even know about yet.

'Today has been a day of many sad things for me. You know Shyamedathi, don't you? I'd not seen her after her son Dineshan was killed. I wanted to go, but didn't have the courage to see her face-to-face when she is so steeped in her sorrow. But I thought it would be wrong to delay it any further, and that's why I went to see her this evening.

'I found her alone on the veranda of her house. She seemed asleep, sitting there below a framed photo of Dineshan with a red garland around it. When she saw me, she tried to give me one of her usual smiles, but her face crumpled and she started crying.

'Unable to speak, we just looked at each other silently. I understood how oppressive silence can be between two people who know all about each other. As we stood there frozen in our misery, Dineshan's father arrived. He was sweating, as if he'd walked a long distance. When he saw me, he smiled happily at me and said, "Ah, Chandutti Mooppan's daughter, aren't you? How's everyone at home? Have you had tea?" And Shyamedathi covered her face and started wailing. The poor man has still not regained the balance of his mind—he still has not registered that his son is gone.

'I took my leave, and came back home to find Vimalechi in a heated argument with Achchan. Sarang and Shanoj stood quietly in a corner, with scared expressions on their faces.

'Dasettan has been discharged from the hospital, and instead of coming here, he has gone to his house with his family. Achchan asked Vimalechi to go there and visit him, which is what started the argument. "I don't have such a husband, and my children don't have a father." I heard Vimalechi shouting through her tears.

'Dasettan seems to have abandoned Vimalechi and, in a way, that's what Vimalechi wanted. So what is behind these tears and commotion? Is marriage a pestilence that one can never get rid of?

'I am not too worried about the situation between Dasettan and Vimalechi. If you ask me, it is best that they separate and live their own lives. What I am worried about is the situation between Valliechi and Hariyettan. Are they still arguing through each night, unable to convince one another? Is Valliechi still punishing Hariyettan by ignoring him and going around dressed in her finery? She hasn't written home even once after they left.'

13.

'I understand what's going on, Comrade,' Krishna told Aravindan, a party activist and neighbour with whom she had never spoken before. 'The District Committee has expelled Ravimaman, accusing him of financial irregularities. That is a low blow. Whatever else he might do, Ravimaman would never embezzle money, nor does he have any need to do so. The real reason is that he had an altercation with a young man at Devu's house. Some people say that he was a regular customer there, and that Maman got into an argument with him. Others say that one of Maman's opponents in the party sent the young man specifically aiming to create trouble. Who knows what the truth is? Anyway, you guys got rid of him very quickly—that was a clever move.

'I wonder what Maman will do now. He lost his job because of his affiliation to the Party, and he spent years working for it, never had a black mark against his name. He's suffered physical assaults, was imprisoned for several months, worked day and night for the Party. And after years of dedicated service, at the age of sixty, he felt an attraction toward a woman. In the beginning, I was a little embarrassed to hear about his new relationship but, thinking about it, I couldn't see anything wrong in it. He is still young at heart and in good health.

'I've only seen this woman Devu once. Shantha pointed her out to me when we went to the festival at Thiyoor temple. Amala and Vineesh had gone to see the animals in the zoo, and I was waiting for them with Valliechi and Hariyettan. Shantha came rushing from somewhere, dragged me aside, and pointed to a woman in a yellow sari standing in front of the magic-show tent.

'"There, that's Devu," she said. "Your Maman's woman."

'She didn't look like a harlot. In fact, she had a quiet beauty. Perhaps she loves Maman more than anyone else, and it would be a good thing. What's the point in spending one's life dreaming about leadership roles and fighting with one's comrades within the party? Wouldn't it be much better to find someone to share the rest of one's life somewhere quiet?

'Aravindan, you might say that I think like this because I have no interest in politics or allegiance to any party. Everything in this country is political, yes, but I think there is something seriously wrong with that.

'You might say that party leaders have a responsibility to be role models, even in their private lives. I am not sure I agree with such a firm stance. And even if you are right, morality is not just about relationships between men and women. It is also about how one goes about accumulating wealth, having a good life, and nursing ambitions about higher and loftier positions. Aren't all party activists affected by these?

'And I am not talking only about the leaders—I am talking also about the ordinary workers and activists. Everyone knows about them and how they have changed. It is not just the leaders who are hoodwinking the people, it is the workers too. Last year, when Valliechi and Hariyettan came home, the auto-rickshaw driver who brought them from town asked for fifty rupees instead of twenty-five. And when Hariyettan challenged him, he got all aggressive and scornful. Do you know who this driver was? None other than Govinnettan's son, Raghu. He is one of your party's regular members. You can't deny that, can you? Oh, you might say, "So what? Those who are ruling us are stealing crores of rupees from us." Well, a crore or five rupees—forcing money out of people is unfair regardless.

'I know, of course, that times have changed, and that people need much more money than before to meet all their needs. But the difference between a good politician and a bad one should be apparent in all walks of lives. Otherwise there is no point in politics at all.

'There is something else I find quite perplexing. When people talk about literature, they say "the author is dead", "the reader is dead", etc. The other day, I went to the town hall for a seminar on history, and there was this young speaker who, at the end of his speech, concluded that history was dead.

'So, if these people are right in thinking that, one by one, everything is dead, what will be left alive in this world? Just some random human beings, animals and plants existing without history or politics or art or literature? Does that mean there will be no difference between human beings and the rest of the world any more? I find myself unable to accept such a proposition. Even if everything else became untrue, won't we, as human beings, retain the ability to feel the pain and pointlessness of our own lives? Or are we to believe that we've lost even that ability? Sometimes, when I think about other people—or even myself, for that matter—I feel that we may have lost this ability after all.'

14.

'I noticed it just this morning,' Krishna said secretly to herself as she stood at the bus stop, waiting for the CMT bus. 'As I was leaving the house this morning, Vimalechi was collecting the laundry, and I noticed a long rip which had been clumsily stitched up at the back of her faded black blouse. It made me want to cry.

'Achchan took care of the household expenses with whatever money he made from selling coconuts, pepper and cashew from our land. And I contribute a share of my salary. Dasettan never took on any responsibility other than buying clothes and things for Vimalechi and the children. Still, we managed. Until

I saw my sister's torn and patched-up blouse, I'd not thought that we weren't well off or that we were, indeed, poor.

'Dasettan has left Vimalechi and the children, and so they are now Achchan's responsibility. I don't have to depend on anyone, and neither should my sister and her children. I won't be able to fulfil all their needs, but we could live together, trying to understand each other and sharing what we have. Perhaps then my sister and I will finally be able to love one another. It's only when the unnecessary knots of life have withered away that love can truly blossom.'

15.

It was Gopan sir who introduced Gloria teacher to Krishna. She'd come to Chethana with her husband.

'Have you met Gloria teacher?'

'No . . .' Krishna had never seen the woman before.

'Teacher is now part of our community,' Gopan sir told her with a laugh that shook his entire body. He introduced her, 'This is Krishna.'

'Where do you live?'

Krishna told her, noting the sweet rhythm of Gloria's voice.

'Oh, so we are neighbours! Do you know Nanu Vaidyar's old house on the south end of the Poothakkavu? I've rented that place.'

Gopan sir told her that Gloria teacher ran a plant nursery. 'She could find you any plant you could ever want,' he said.

Krishna studied the woman who'd come to Theeyoor to sell plants. She had short bob-cut hair, a pretty round face, full lips red with lipstick, and thin eyebrows. She wore a single string of black beads around her neck, and a pair of oversized hoops in her ears. The purple sari and sleeveless blouse suited her fair skin. She became conscious that Gloria was examining her with an equally interested look. This made her uncomfortable.

'Come home when you have some time. I've only been here a week and I'm bored already! I haven't found anyone suitable to spend time with yet.'

As they talked, Jitesh walked in, gave them a look and went away. Later, it was he who told her all about Gloria teacher. She was the daughter of a school teacher named Peter in Chenkara. As a young girl, she had been a gifted singer and, when she was sixteen, she'd run away with a musician to Mangalapuram. He had some sort of work there. By the time he left her and moved on, she had found herself a job as a music teacher in a school. When that was over, she'd worked in a beauty parlour. At that time, she'd taken up with a mechanic. That relationship hadn't lasted long either, and now she was with a third man. She had no children. Having returned to Chenkara around four or five years ago, she ran a beauty parlour from her house, before setting up the nursery business.

Gloria teacher was an unusual woman, Jitesh told Krishna. She was not scared of anyone, especially men. From the way he talked about her, it was clear that Jitesh considered Gloria to be a bad woman. Asha and Reshma were trying not to laugh out loud as he spoke.

The next day—a Sunday—Krishna woke up feeling a curious sense of dejection. Her mind was preoccupied with thoughts of Shantha, Dineshan and Divakaran; she dwelled on the fact that they had all left this world, and it made her sad. Faraway faces of others who had been her classmates in school and college came to her, and she wondered where they might be and what their lives would be like. She marvelled at the fact that, although she would have met thousands of people in her life, she knew about the lives of only a handful of them. Where were the rest of them? When did they disappear down the many lanes of life? She acknowledged the painful thought that, as far as she was concerned, the world was a very small place, and that she had only a handful of memories to call her own.

She sat frozen within these thoughts until afternoon. She had a late lunch. After her shower, as she did her laundry, she thought about Gloria teacher and decided to visit her. As she set out in her street clothes, unusual for a Sunday, Achchan asked her, 'Where are you off to?'

'Oh, not far. To visit a teacher.'

Beyond the dirt road, as she walked down the slope toward Poothakkavu, she saw two young men emerge out of the woods. 'Drunkards,' she said to herself, slightly afraid. She had heard talk that the Poothakkavu had become a hangout for such people lately.

One of the young men had a vertical line of kunkumam on his forehead, and the other had a brass bangle on his wrist. They had their arms around each other and walked on unsteady feet. As Krishna passed them, one of them said, 'What do you reckon? First-class material or what?'

'Absolutely. The back view is even better.'

'A1 seating capacity. Oh, mate, I can barely contain myself.'

Their loud, loose laugh made Krishna sick, her body felt weightless as though all her organs had disappeared from within it. She hurried along, dragging the husk of her body blowing in the wind, and did not dare look back fearing that those strange men might be following her. Her only consolation was that she could see Gloria teacher's house from where she was. She allowed herself to look back only when she reached the front gate. The men hadn't followed her—they were gone, having said whatever came to their mouth in their drunken brazenness. It was nothing new; she'd had to put up with such nastiness before. In any case, she needn't have been that scared. These were not deserted places any more—there were a few houses within earshot.

Krishna opened the gate and entered Gloria teacher's house. Her husband was in the front yard among the plants, a pair of shears in his hand. Taking in his t-shirt with NEWYORKER printed on it and his ridiculous Bermuda shorts, Krishna suppressed a smile.

Gloria teacher sat on a wicker chair on the veranda, busy with some needlework. She looked younger and prettier in her light blue embroidered maxi. Upon seeing Krishna, she called out, 'Hi,' and got up with a big smile.

'Vincent, you remember, we met Krishna at Gopan sir's college.'

Her husband smiled and nodded, and turned back to his plants.

'Come, let's go inside,' Gloria teacher said and led the way.

It had been at least twenty years since Krishna had been inside this house. With a start, Krishna remembered that the last time she was here was when Nanu Vaidyar killed himself by hanging himself from its rafter. She and Shantha had sneaked in without permission, eager to see what a suicide by hanging looked like but, by the time they got here, the body had been cut loose and there was a crowd of people around it.

That was the first suicide Krishna remembered. Since then,

the house had never been constantly occupied. Nanu Vaidyar's children were all grown up and lived in other parts of the country, and took very little interest in managing the house or renting it out. On the rare occasions when it was rented out, it was through his younger brother.

'Something to drink?' Gloria teacher asked her.

'Thanks. I am okay.'

'No, no. It's your first visit. Give me two minutes, I'll make some coffee.' Gloria teacher went into the kitchen.

Krishna looked at the calendar on the wall, with the picture of a kingfisher sitting forlorn on a wooden post by a river.

'Come into the kitchen, Krishna,' Gloria teacher called out. 'There's no one else here.'

'Come, sit,' Gloria teacher said as she entered the kitchen. She set a pot of water on the stove for the coffee.

'What does your husband do?' Krishna asked.

'Husband?' Gloria teacher laughed. 'No, no. He is my helper. Like you, everyone thinks Vincent is my husband.' Leaning on her shoulder, she whispered into her ears, 'He can't do what a husband is required to do.' Her entire body shook as she laughed at her own joke. Krishna felt uncomfortable, but Gloria teacher didn't seem to notice and attended to the coffee.

Teacher served the coffee in light blue cups. As she drank it, she touched Krishna's hair gently and arranged it a little lower on her forehead.

'You have a lovely heart-shaped face,' Gloria teacher said. 'Comb your hair a little lower like this. It looks better that way. Otherwise your forehead looks big.'

Gloria teacher pinched her chin lightly. Krishna felt somewhat irritated by her blatant familiarity.

'You're unmarried, aren't you?' Gloria teacher asked. 'Gopan sir told me. It's good that way. Look at me. I married twice and got rid of both of them. Men are boring. I have no need for their help.'

After coffee, Gloria teacher led Krishna outside. The yard was full of plants in planters, pots, and plastic containers of various sizes and shapes. Hibiscus, orchids, roses, anthuriums, lilies, and a hundred others whose names Krishna didn't know.

'It's only been a couple of days since we brought all of these over. I haven't had the time to arrange them properly,' Gloria teacher told Krishna, and took her to the south end of the yard where there was a variety of saplings in little plastic pots—banyan, mango, bamboo, pine, bougainvillea . . .

'Here, look, this is a bonsai. I have around fifty of them,' Gloria said. 'It's the loving labour of a very long time.' Her face was suffused with a childlike pride, and Krishna felt a kind of affection for her.

'Come, Krishna, over here,' Gloria said, kneeling in front of a plant pot. There was a plant that looked to Krishna like a gooseberry. She sat down next to Gloria, expecting her to talk about the plant. Instead, Gloria suddenly hugged Krishna and, moving her hair out of the way, kissed her on the nape of her neck with a hissing sound.

Something crawled all over Krishna's body. She scrambled up and rushed through the front yard and, by the time she was out of the gate, she was almost running.

The sun was on its way down.

As she walked home panting, the lane along the Poothakkavu was dim with shadows. Krishna felt that there were dense forests in front of her, behind her and around her, closing in on her from all sides. She felt the desperate urge to talk about something—anything—to rescue herself from the feeling of being engulfed. But what she muttered, as she struggled to breathe, was this: 'Yes, forests. Definitely forests.'

Adrshyavanangal, 1998

diary of a malayali madman

Preface

I have been working on a novel for five or six years. Every so often I'd feel that it was not going the way I intended and then I'd stop, consider another structure, and start writing, only to feel, again, that I was going down the wrong path. A few months later, after many such starts and stops, I settled on a structure that seemed to work and began writing diligently. I had completed four or five chapters when, one night, a madman, one who had no connection whatsoever to the novel's atmosphere or storyline, came to my mind, bringing with him an array of random musings. I was somewhat taken aback, but I also felt a surge of excitement and—I am not quite sure how—I remembered Gogol. I had a copy of his book, *St. Petersburg Stories*, which contained the story, 'Diary of a Madman'. It took some effort to locate it among the piles of books strewn around the house. I read the story again and was satisfied that there was no relationship between Gogol's madman and mine, and that the incidents that had entered my mind—those worthy of inclusion in the story—had no similarities with the experiential world of Gogol's madman. There was no cause for concern. So I started writing in earnest. I don't remember writing anything else with the ease or speed with which I have written this story.

Before passing your judgement on 'Diary of a Malayali Madman', know this: the protagonist of this story has already forgotten about this diary. He is currently immersed in work of a philosophical nature. Respected reader, I will take you there in due course. Let me stop for now.

– N. Prabhakaran

20 August 2012, Monday

Hahaha . . . Look at the title I've given to my diary: 'Diary of a Malayali Madman'. Hahaha . . . Only a Malayali madman can write his diary in Malayalam, and only a Malayali can read it. Obviously, one can learn a new language, read and write in it. I was only talking about the normal state of affairs. You understand, don't you? Let that be. Have you heard of a writer named Gogol? It is unlikely, if you are below the age of thirty. People below thirty are generally ignorant. They may have a degree or two, but when it comes to general knowledge they have none. There's no way they would have heard of Gogol. In actual fact, Gogol is a great literary figure. Here, in Kerala, most people say they like Dostoevsky, or perhaps Tolstoy. Me, I like this fellow Gogol. Anyway, my intention is not to get into a literary discussion. The reason I thought of Gogol just now is because he has written a story called 'Diary of a Madman'. It is this work of his that inspired me to write this diary. But there is one important difference. Gogol's hero does not think of himself as mad. Even when he imagines things that other people would consider completely insane, he doesn't think there is anything wrong with his state of mind. My situation is different—I am a little bit mad, and I am quite aware of this without having to be told. Given that I have this much self-awareness, you may also consider me quite sane. That's all up to you.

This is intended to be a diary, but I've started writing it as if it were a story. So let's continue in that vein for a while. I don't need to specify that I am the hero of this story. The heroines are several, and I will tell you about them as and when the context demands. First, let me introduce myself properly. I have a polytechnic diploma in mechanical engineering. After completing this course, I went to Bangalore and drifted around for a while. Nothing good came out of it. So I went to Mumbai. I have an uncle who, having returned home filthy rich after spending forty-odd years in Mumbai, goes around pretending that he is a community leader because he is the president of the local temple committee. Through one of his acquaintances, he got me a job in Mumbai as an apprentice in a scooter company, complete with rent-free accommodation. Listening to him go on about it, you'd think I had won the lottery. I didn't know how much I'd be paid, and when I came to know, I couldn't believe it! How was one to survive in that megacity on such a low salary? I had no idea, and I said as much to my uncle.

'You have to train for one year. Is it right to demand a one-lakh-rupee salary as soon as you get there? I did roadwork for one rupee when I first went to Mumbai. Put up with it if you can. If not, come back home and squander away your life getting drunk and what not.'

I didn't listen to his advice and promptly left the job. Let me not go into the difficulties I faced afterward. Eventually, I found a well-run workshop with a decent owner. Weekly wages, okay salary, and he seemed to really like me. There was a tiny, cage-like room behind the workshop. I cooked, ate and slept in it for six years, sharing the space with a Bengali lad. Then my relatives and people back home started saying that I should get married. I tried to look for girls with good jobs, but didn't find anyone I liked. So I decided to select one from a well-to-do family and found a suitable girl with an ordinary BA degree. Her degree was in sociology, but she was completely ignorant of social sciences, history or geography. Ask her where China is, and she'd say it is near Nigeria! Nevertheless, she put on terrible airs. She'd studied in English-medium schools and could speak good enough English—definitely better than me. Still, no basic knowledge and, on top of that, she had a habit of saying something foolish and then going on and on about it.

One night, on our honeymoon—on the fourth day after our wedding—she started arguing with me saying that Leonardo da Vinci was born after C.V. Raman. That argument ended in a divorce. In the heat of the argument, I said some things that should not have been said, some bad, no, outright obscene words. That became an issue. Oh, I started writing a diary entry and now seem to be writing my autobiography. No, that's not what this is about.

21 August, Tuesday

I felt lethargic from the moment I got up this morning and had planned to just stay at home today. But, at ten in the morning, my sister and brother-in-law dropped in. My brother-in-law gave me a good telling off for squandering away my time, not taking up a job, and hanging around political activists. He showed no consideration for the fact that I am a forty-some-thing man. My sister also joined in and said a few things. Let them—let everyone say whatever they want. It doesn't concern me. I have my path; they have theirs.

In fact, my brother-in-law is mistaken in his opinion that I hang around political activists. Actually, they don't pay any attention to me and I don't take them seriously. I go to their meetings sometimes, just for fun. As a listener, that's all. I like those leaders who have a certain oratory style and speak gesticulating wildly with their hands and feet. I don't care what their political affiliations are or which factions they belong to. I get goosebumps when I listen to them speak. The other day, at the Congress Party meeting in Kottayi bazaar, I stopped one of the leaders on his way to the stage and said, 'Brother, rock it.' And he rocked it. I think he may have been under the influence. Having worked himself up with his own enthusiasm, he began to have a go at an opponent he had within his own party:

'I'll gut him if he takes issue with me,' he said. 'I will squeeze out his liver, add it to lemonade and drink it.'

This was greeted with thunderous applause from the audience. I also applauded.

There is another thing. In my part of the world, unlike in the olden days, there is no great rivalry between politicians from different parties. They're all businessmen. Come election time, they pretend to be arch-rivals like snakes and mongooses. Behind the scenes, though, there are many 'adjustments'. Let that be. There's no point in wishing that these things should not happen. So let them carry on, isn't that better? There was an incident the other day. It was around ten or eleven in the morning, and I was sitting in the chai shop near the jetty. Some young politicians walked in—city folk, by the look of it—representing parties on both the left and the right. None of them knew me, except perhaps vaguely recognizing my face from somewhere. There's been some controversy around the sale of a ten-acre property belonging to Dubai Avullakka, and these looked like mediators who'd come to find a solution. In situations such as these, the mediators receive a set percentage of the sale price as commission. They seemed quite beside themselves with the excitement of it all.

'Yes, send twelve to the District Committee. Hand it to Dingan, he knows where and how to give it. Eh? That guy's case? Call the Mumbai-wallah and tell him. He'll take care of it. Avullakka's problem? That's why we're here first thing in the morning, isn't it, to get it solved.' A khaddar-clad youngster, clean, wholesome, and full of youthful enthusiasm and energy, talked with great self-importance into a mobile phone as big as a diary. There was no one else in the shop except me, and Chandrettan who made the tea. As he hung up, one of his friends asked me with a sour smile on his face:

'Brother, do you mind if we hung around here for a while and had some brandy?'

It was quite clear that he was having me on—his voice and overall demeanour reflected the heavy weight of sarcasm.

'What do you reckon?' I asked him. 'This shop belongs to Kocha Nanuvettan. Some tosspot politicians like you beat him up and broke his left leg when he went to picket a brandy shop during the prohibition campaign. You think you can come into his shop and ask such vulgar questions?'

Baduvathi the Cat was lying asleep under the bench. She woke up just then, and came out and said to them, 'Better clear off quickly. My husband Kandan Kannan will soon be here, and if he catches sight of you, he'll cut off your cockles. He hates alcohol.' As soon as they heard her, they fled. I couldn't stop laughing, seeing them panic and scramble. But my laughter seems to have annoyed Chandrettan.

'Why are you laughing, Aagi?' he asked.

'I was laughing at what the Cat said, and the way those politicians ran away.'

'What cat? What politicians? What the heck are you going on about, Aagi?'

So Chandrettan was not aware of anything that had happened there.

This is the problem with our country, as far as I can figure out. No one sees anything. No one hears anything.

Ah, and one more thing. Chandrettan called me 'Aagi'. I am sure you'd be keen to know my name.

My name is Aagney, which means son of Agni, the fire god. My father was a teacher and a Sanskrit scholar. My mother was a nurse. I've heard it said that the biggest mistake my father made was to marry my mother. My mother does not know Sanskrit. She is always angry. It must have been all the hard work at the hospital, anger has become her default position. Nurses have really hard jobs—it's not without reason that they are always on strike. My mother was a nurse in a government hospital, so she had a good salary. Now she has a very good pension. That is why I can afford to walk around in these ironed shirts and trousers.

So today got over like that. Well, not quite. Because Chandrettan said to me, 'Aagi, why don't you go home and take your medicine?'

I got pissed off so I shouted at him, 'What medicine? Whose medicine? Ask your woman to take her medicine.'

To be fair, that last bit was uncalled for. So what happened? Chandrettan rushed at me and slapped my face. I slapped him right back. He didn't give in. So we stopped with the slapping and started fighting in earnest. Some people came running and pulled us apart, so both of us got out of it without much damage. But I think I've sprained my neck, and my left arm is in some pain too. I'll have to get it massaged by Kumaran Vaidyar tomorrow. Yet another expense to worry about.

22 August, Wednesday

My plan was to go back to Mumbai after my wedding and bring my wife over within three months. I'd even looked for suitable accommodation for us. But when she left, thoughts of Mumbai also left me. For a couple of years after that, I worked in a local car company's service station. After that, I spent some time doing odd-jobs, repair work and such. I am not quite sure why I'm recalling all these things and writing them down here. What a pity . . . I wish I could write something literary. Since leaving high school, I had not even touched a Malayalam book until three years ago. I was going through a period of great distress—I was even scared that I'd lose my mental balance. That's when my brother-in-law took me to a clinical psychologist—Dr Subodh Kumar at the Specialty Hospital. He was a good man. He talked to me at length over several days. He's the one who persuaded me to start reading novels and short stories. After that, I just read and read and that was really helpful.

As my reading progressed, I began to feel that I should get acquainted with writers and theatre people. I met some in person and had telephone conversations with some others.

Compared to the people at the places where I used to work, these literary people have several good qualities. For one thing, they seem to grasp quickly things that many others would never be able to understand. But commonalities aside, they are as varied as any other group of human beings. Among them are the good, the malevolent, the conceited, the clever, the extremely vulnerable, the crooks, the helpers, the cultured, and the rogues. At the mere hint of any situation that may cause personal harm or threat to them, they tend to withdraw rather quickly—some make strange arguments, while others slink away quietly. This tendency for self-preservation seems to be the other commonality among them. You must forgive me for saying these things about our highly respected literary figures.

23 August, Thursday

I'm not writing in my diary today. I've not signed a contract that I'll write every day without fail, have I? Come to think of it, what is the point of this writing?

26 August, Sunday

I didn't venture out today. In the morning, I read Kumaranasan's poem *Chintaavishtayaaya Sita* and found myself disagreeing with several sections. In the evening, I read the book *How to Get Rich in 30 Days* and found that I had no disagreements with anything.

1 September, Saturday

Today, I had a discussion about the future of communism with Gokulan. He was adamant that the Indian bourgeoisie was comprador-bourgeoisie. I was not keen to get into an argument with him, but also didn't want him to think that I was an ignoramus. So I said that Indian communists were all kulaks.

3 September, Monday

I met a lad named Avinash today. He's completed BTech but has no job yet. He told me all about his future plans. He wanted to join a 'quotation gang', go to Mumbai and get acquainted with some underworld heroes and, after working with them and making a name for himself, come back home and explore his options with the leaders of local factions.

As we were talking, a crow came and sat on a branch of the mango tree. 'A goonda by the name of Mushugopi will strangle this lad to death in about three years' time,' the crow said to me.

I didn't tell Avinash what the crow said. You can never be certain about human destiny. Things may not pan out as the crow said. This lad might actually get involved with quotation gangs for a while and then stand for elections representing some political party and reach the parliament. He might become a member of a peace committee sent to soothe some local conflict and make a name for himself. He might eventually win some awards for peace. For all you know, he might even receive the Nobel Peace Prize.

4 September, Tuesday

This evening, as I walked through the town, I saw a beautiful young woman. Not fat, not too skinny either. I fancied her and wanted to see her up close. But as I was crossing the road, a bus arrived, and she got in and left. The bus was going toward Manthodi. I felt certain that she lived in Manthodi and that her house would be in the vicinity of the Sree Krishna temple. It was another half hour before the next bus to Manthodi. I got on the bus and got off at Upper Manthodi stop and walked straight to the temple. I was absolutely certain that she would have gone home, had a bath and gone into the temple. Soon it was dark, but there was no sign of her. Several other women went in and out of the temple.

I was standing there feeling dejected, when a middle-aged man came toward me. Kunkumam on the forehead, saffron mundu, no shirt—undoubtedly a protector of the Hindu religion. I felt very scared.

The man asked me in a grave voice, 'Where are you from?' I told him the name of my village.

He looked at me as if he didn't believe me. 'Name?' he asked.

'Aagney,' I answered, also with proper gravity. That seemed to pique his interest in me.

'Would you like some paayasam?' he asked.

Before I could reply, he said, 'I'm forty-eight years old. My wife is forty-two. We've been married for twenty years, but it was only last week that she gave birth to our first child. It is the result of all the prayers and offerings we made at this temple in the last year and a half. This temple has great divine power. We might think that all trees are the same, but some, as you may know, are special—the peepal, the sacred wood apple, the eranhi, the venga. In the same way, temples may all seem the same, but some are special. You must have seen temples in some places that are like colicky children. Why do you think that is? They lack divine power, that's why. Well, you mustn't leave without having some paayasam.'

Saying this, he went back inside the temple, and I ran away from there like lightning.

7 September, Friday

It must have been around 11 AM I was in town, doing nothing in particular. I only had six rupees in my possession. If I had six more, I could have had some tea and plantain fritters. This thought made me sad. I'd borrowed five thousand rupees from my mother as soon as she received her pension. I felt strongly that it wasn't right to spend more than that in a month, especially since I was getting free food at home. But five thousand rupees would stretch only until about the twentieth of the month. I have no idea where the money disappears. I don't smoke, drink or have relations with women. I take the bus a lot, have tea in various chai shops and watch an occasional film—that's pretty much it. Oh, and I call people on my mobile phone, but that comes to only about a thousand rupees a month. Yet, five thousand rupees disappear like steam within twenty days. The mystery behind this was explained to me by a palm-reader I met at the kaavu festival. Apparently, my hands leak! It is true; I have hands like a sieve. No matter how many thousands I have, they'll just flow out of my hands. She said I had a good heart. She also said that I was still burdened with the sorrow of being jilted by a woman. She even recited a verse beginning with, 'Of women born . . .' This palm-reader was very pretty. I considered running away with her after the festival fireworks. What a lovely life that would be, nomadic, spending time at one festival ground after another! But what can you say other than hard luck—she already had a husband, one with a big, spiky moustache. An ugly man, with teeth stained red from paan. His lips were a horrible dirty red too. He was not a suitable match for her at all, but what to do—he was her husband.

I was going to write about something else . . . Ah, yes, I remember. So, as I was standing there, feeling dejected that I didn't have enough money for plantain fritters, a young chap carrying a heavy-looking bag came and stood before me.

'Sir, do you like to read?' he asked in a respectful tone. No one had called me 'sir' in a very long time. I was so happy that I almost entered a state of bliss.

He pulled me back from that state. As if in a dream, I saw him take out a book from his bag.

'This is my first collection of poetry, sir. You must buy a copy and help me.'

I feigned interest and accepted the proffered book.

The title of the book was *The Crocodiles of Lake Mava*. I knew from the first glance that it wasn't for me, but I didn't let him see my disinterest.

'Sorry, I forgot to pick up my purse when I left home this morning. And I don't like to borrow money. I only have enough for the bus fare home.'

'Oh, that doesn't matter, sir. I'll get bus tickets for both of us, and let's go to your house. That way, we can sit there and have an undisturbed discussion about poetry for a while.'

I couldn't wriggle out of it, and so he came home with me. My poet friend will never understand the pain I felt in having to borrow one hundred rupees from my mother.

'The book costs eighty-five rupees, but I'm only taking sixty-five from you, sir,' he said, giving thirty-five rupees back to me.

I think it was quickly apparent to him that my house didn't have an environment conducive to reciting poetry or discussing literature. In any case, he left pretty soon. He asked me if I liked to drink alcohol and I said no, which may also have encouraged him to leave promptly.

I didn't have the courage to ask my mother to offer this young poet some tea. In this world, the only experience that someone with no personal income or means has in abundance is self-loathing.

11 September, Tuesday

Saturday the 8th was a horrible day. I received a terrible beating on that day, the pain and soreness of which have only just started abating. That is why I have not written in this diary for the last few days.

Saturday morning was actually quite peaceful. After having tea in the morning, I tried reading *The Crocodiles of Lake Mava* but couldn't make head or tail of it. To be honest, I didn't understand a single one of the thirty-seven poems in that book. Why, I didn't even understand where or what Lake Mava was! Of course, no one can understand everything in this world. Even this diary of mine will be incomprehensible to many people. This world—this universe—is structured that way. Why does the gooseberry tree have such small leaves? Why does the lapwing have yellow wattles on both sides of its beak? What purpose does the unwieldy body of the hippopotamus serve? Would it have been wrong for it to have a simpler, more elegant body? Is there a rule to all this? Who decides what one animal should look like and what the other shouldn't? Is it nature? Is nature capable of making such independent decisions? There must be someone beyond nature who controls it—someone who could be thought of as God. I have no faith in God's justice. My reckoning is that good people—people who are by nature incapable of doing bad things—don't succeed in life.

As a rule, I don't trust people who are successful. I feel that there'd be lot of tactics, trickery and treachery behind every successful life. Maybe there are a handful of people who are not so—the lucky few, perhaps two to three per cent of those who are successful. Be that as it may.

I sat at home immersed in such thoughts until about four in the afternoon, and then took the bus into town. Leaving the noisy crowded streets behind, I walked along the quieter back-streets. The interior of the town is almost a village—our town is just the outer shell of the village. A few ramshackle houses and shops, two or three kaavu, some mosques, big and small, an old church, an ancient cemetery . . . I've seen these sights several times, but they never lose their appeal. As I walked along, taking all this in, I saw a goat with a profoundly sorrowful expression tethered to the side of the road. A few leafy twigs of the jackfruit tree were strewn in front of him. He was munching away, but I could see that he was in some distress.

'What's the matter, friend?' I asked.

'I've been brought to a wedding house nearby,' the goat told me. 'They will slaughter me for the feast tomorrow.'

It was quite possible that he was telling the truth, but what could I do? Broadly speaking, people like to have some meat on special occasions. Forget about the vegetarians who are any-way only a minority. What is a meat-eating human to do? Meat doesn't grow on trees. You have to kill living things to get it. Killing is a sin. Once upon a time, school children used to prac-tise handwriting with the sentence: *Konnal paapam thinnal theerum* (The sin of slaughtering an animal is assuaged by the eating of its meat). Killing is allowed if it is for food. Snake kills frog; lion kills deer; tiger kills boar—you can observe a whole series of such killings in nature. Oh . . . I don't understand the logic in any of this. If the lion has the right to live, doesn't the deer have it too? Of course, I have also heard the rationalizations: if animals didn't kill each other, there'd be no more space on this earth; there'd be no more natural resources; no one would have enough to eat. These rationalizations are at once logical and illogical. Anyway . . . Suffice it to say that it was my bad luck that I stopped to talk to that goat, and stood there perplexed.

A small crowd of about eight to ten people surrounded me, saying that I was standing there with the intention of stealing that goat. Apparently, goat-poaching had been going on in that area for some time. I really was not expecting such a turn of events. They said I gave inconsistent answers to their questions about my whereabouts. I'm not sure if that is true, but if it is, there could be two reasons for it: one, I may have been extremely scared, or, two, I may have decided to pull their legs. Either way, the outcome was the same: I got beaten senseless. Then they pushed and prodded and dragged me off to the police station. There were only two policemen at the station. I guessed that one of them must be the station-writer; the other was a young lad who looked as if he'd joined the police force only yesterday. I know nothing about police ranks and designations and all that stuff. There was no sub-inspector or other senior officers at the station.

The policemen talked to the people who brought me there and asked them to write down in detail all that had happened. They said that the statement should be addressed to the sub-inspector and signed by all present.

Then the policeman who may have been the station-writer said, 'You people have seriously worked this guy over. You do know that the public have no right to beat up the accused. That's the job of the police.'

As soon as he said this, more than half the people who brought me there slunk away. The rest started shouting and arguing with the writer-policeman. And that's when the sub-inspector and two other policemen came in. Suddenly, everyone quieted down.

'What's the problem?' The SI's voice resonated like that of an actor on stage. I had goosebumps. No one spoke. Then the writer-policeman spoke up:

'Theft, sir.' He pointed at me and said, 'He tried to steal a goat.'

'Is that true?' the SI asked me.

'No, sir.'

'What then?'

I described everything that had happened in great detail. I'm not quite sure why, but everyone at the station, including the SI, burst out laughing.

'This guy is your goat-thief?' the SI asked the people who had brought me there. Then he pointed to his forehead and said, 'There should be some life up here. Otherwise you'll continue accusing random people of goat-theft and dragging them to the police station. Do you get what I'm saying? Now get out of my face. Go!' With a flick of his hand, he sent everyone away.

I felt very happy. What a nice SI! I didn't know that such good policemen existed. As I was thinking this, he beckoned to me. I'd just reached his table when he grabbed me by my neck.

'Go on, get lost,' he said, shoving me hard. 'Go home and

stay put. Who do you think you are? God? Going around taking care of grief-stricken goats and chicken . . .'

I heard that much as I got up from where I had fallen and
walked away.

Even now, as I am writing this, I am struggling to understand why he pushed me like that and said such things. So
many things happen in this world that we'll never be able to
comprehend.

12 September, Wednesday

I met a famous multilingual scholar today. He'd taught in many
Indian and international universities. He was over eighty years
of age, but still seemed as energetic as a young man. Elegant
body, lustrous eyes, fulsome lips flushed red as if from the pas-
sion of a thousand interests. (Hey, look how lyrical my language has become from reading all those literary works.)

In response to my question about the origins of the
Malayalam language, he started talking about several difficult
issues in the ancient history of Kerala: the hundred-year war,
the feudal system, the matrilineal tradition of inheritance . . . As
he went on talking, the professor disappeared and, in his place,
I saw an enormous rooster. This was no ordinary local rooster.
I remembered having seen a similar rooster before, early one
morning in Belgaum, standing with his head held high on top
of a nomadic group's piled-up bags and bundles.

'Well, Rooster, what are you doing here?' I asked.

'Eh? What's that?' asked the professor, alarmed.

'Oh, it's nothing, sir. As I was looking at you, I saw a big
rooster. I was just saying hello.'

Before I could finish, the rooster began crowing loudly, as

if possessed. He scratched up some dirt with his nails, flicked it into my eyes and, spreading his wings, ran swiftly away. I was disappointed that my conversation with the professor was disrupted, but felt happy to have met the rooster.

15 September, Saturday

When I woke up from my afternoon nap, I felt like writing a few lines of poetry. Even the title came to me promptly: 'The Insane'. So then I had no option but to write. Here is the poem I wrote. Read carefully.

> The insane is unfortunate
> The moonlight and the worm that crawls in it
> Are all the same to him
> He can reach into the Sun
> But swiftly withdraws his hand
> Grabs a piece of darkness and chews on it
> Like sugarcane, drinking in its juice
> He breaks fast with God
> And dines with the Devil
> Oh, tough is the fate of the insane.

Utter crap, isn't it? I thought so too.

16 September, Sunday

I reread the book *How to Get Rich in 30 Days*.

I felt I must, somehow or the other, become a rich man. Why, exactly, are the poor and the hapless even alive? To be honest, they don't deserve to live. A human being must somehow make some money, and there are plenty of ways to do this: real estate, social service with international funding, benami deals for the leaders of top political parties, organizing sectarian activities disguised as cultural events for communal factions, transforming oneself into a guru to help foreigners in spiritual crises, and so on and so forth. Just become an expert in any one of these—problem solved. It's quite easy actually.

17 September, Monday

There's a big peepal tree on the south end of the bus stop in town. If it weren't for the local environmentalists, it would have been chopped down years ago.

Every Monday evening, a man around seventy years old appears under the tree. His normal attire is a pair of dirty pyjamas and a kurta. In the three years I have seen him here, I've never seen these clothes in a clean condition. He doesn't speak to anyone. He only opens his mouth once every fifteen minutes, and when he does, he points the forefinger of his right hand up, down, left and right, and says, 'There I am. There I am.' He repeats this three times and then goes silent for another fifteen minutes. Meanwhile, the assembled onlookers murmur, 'Om, Om', sounding like an enormous swarm of hornets. I asked a few people what all this meant, but got a reply only from two people. I understood nothing of the first guy's response except for a few familiar words such as God, Brahmam, cosmos and so on. The rest was gobbledygook.

The other guy told me, 'It's quite simple, my friend. This kurta-wallah cannot see anyone or anything except himself. Isn't that the kind of existence everyone craves these days? Not having to care for or love or be benevolent to anyone, not having to get involved ... This guy has reached the highest level of such an existence. If not such a person, who else are we going to idolize?'

Having said this much, he pointed the forefinger of his right hand up, down, left and right as if doing an exercise, and said, 'There I am, there I am.'

I was scared, watching his eyes bulge out of their sockets.

18 September, Tuesday

To become rich, one should first be able to achieve stability of mind. One must liberate one's mind from all other thoughts and concentrate solely on the aim of making money.

Why do we get an education?

Why do we expand our skills?

Why do we get involved in politics?

Why do we pursue a literary life?

Why does a doctor treat a patient?

Why do people express moral outrage about stuff?

The answer to all these questions is the same: for money.

All human beings must understand the significance of wealth. Until a person attains the pinnacle of such an under-standing, that person is not truly alive.

I began to comprehend this simple matter only after read-ing the preface to the book *How to Get Rich in 30 Days* several times over and digesting its message.

It is quite possible that such poppycock colours many of the insights in this world. Consider the pronouncements made by spiritual gurus who have no financial worries, who never have to deal with opposition from politicians or any-one else. It is all meaningless blather. Let them try fending for themselves, doing some ordinary job to provide for their own food, shelter and clothing. Then they'll understand that irresponsibly mouthing off as they do is equal to committing mortal sin.

And there's one more thing. The followers of these spiritual gurus—the trusting believers—they are no squares either. They are proper worshippers of wealth and prestige. Imagine, for a second, that one of these spiritual leaders, male or female, declared: 'I don't want money or followers, Indian or foreign. I don't want buildings constructed in my name. I don't want the support of any community or political party. I don't need anything other than spiritual bliss.' Imagine, then, that they started living as they said. What do you think will happen? No one will even turn and look at them.

Are you beginning to feel bored? I am feeling quite bored too. Some days are like that, one's mind goes scuttling after some boring topic.

It is noon now. Best time to catch some sleep.

19 September, Wednesday

There was an Urdu play at the town hall today, performed by a troupe from Delhi. I don't remember whose play it was, or what it was about. There were just two characters, both women. One was in a folk-dancer costume: a white skirt with small, brown flowers reaching just below the knee, a maroon top with a dark blue vest over it, and a necklace and glass bangles adorned with sparkly stones. The second woman was dressed like a Rajasthani dancer in a long multicoloured skirt and a dark red scarf. There were more songs and dances than actual dialogue. Their dance had a wonderful rhythm—from the tip of their fingers to every atom in their body, they seemed to be celebrating the beauty of movement.

As I sat there watching the play, I began to feel terribly sad. I felt that the rhythm of this dance would never be repeated in quite this way ever again. Even these same performers wouldn't be able to repeat this performance. These singers and musicians would never come together with these same emotions ever again. This play will end here—today. Some people may have made a video recording of it, but that would be a different visual experience. I continued thinking such thoughts and my sadness increased. Sitting in the dark hall, I began to weep quietly. Then, suddenly, I had a strange thought. This dance does not end here. It will remain in the atmosphere. Or the particles of this dance will come together in some part of the atmosphere. There, on an invisible and unknowable stage, this dance will continue eternally. The future—many futures—will receive their dance, while remaining unaware of it. This thought made me exceedingly happy. The performers continued dancing to the alternating beats of gypsy and Rajasthani music. I couldn't contain my joy any longer.

I got up on a chair and shouted, 'Arre, wah wah,' and applauded the performers.

Someone shouted from behind, 'Sit down, you!' I was not scared of him, but I sat down anyway.

20 September, Thursday

I had a long chat with God today about a lot of things—especially about His existence.

'I am what you want me to be,' God told me. 'You can define me however you like—you could choose to use incomprehensible words or simple transparent language. I don't care. I have no particular demands or desires. You are the one who should decide who I am. You need me to love and to hate, to praise and to vilify, to frighten and to get rid of fear. That will do for now. If you ever consider doing a PhD in philosophy or theology, we can continue this discussion in a more abstruse language.'

'Oh, God, have I landed myself in trouble?' I thought to myself and ran away. I am in a precarious state as it is, and definitely don't want to create a situation where God takes it upon himself to mess things up further for me.

8 November, Thursday

I have been in a terrible state for the last forty days or so. You must have heard of Kandaka Shani—the transit of Saturn that rains bad luck on people. I'm not sure if the calamity it brings is usually so short-lived—I haven't consulted an astrologer—but it seems to me that I have been hit by it and it is only this morning that I have managed to come out of it. Sukumaran sir and Jayanth have been trying to get me out on bail for the last two days, and the good magistrate finally sanctioned bail at 11 AM this morning. May good come upon everyone!

Let me tell you what happened in detail. It all began on 21 September when, at the market, I met a saffron-clad, strikingly handsome sanyasi. I don't think I have ever seen a face so beautiful and alive. I was standing on the footpath under this foreign divi-divi tree. Perhaps he noticed my appreciative looks, he came and stood directly in front of me, straight as a needle, and with no apparent change in his facial expression, said:

'Tell me, Shishya, what do you desire? Do you wish to live in a palace with a beautiful princess? Would you like to conquer some country and rule over it? Or perhaps you'd rather travel the distant oceans, alone in a sailing ship? Tell me, and I will make it happen.'

'Oh-ho, just my kind of guy,' I thought and, gladly prostrating myself before him, said:

'Guru, I don't know how to thank you for this affection you shower upon me. However, I do not desire any of these things.'

'What then? What do you want?'

'I would like some mental peace—a milligram will do.'

'Oh, my dear Shishya, you're truly sensible. One milligram—or as they say in our local parlance, a pinch of mental peace—that's the very thing that is most prized in this universe. I have travelled all around the world advising millions of people on how to attain true happiness. There's nothing as easy in this world as dishing out advice. But let me tell you, my dear friend, this thing that you desire, a pinch of mental peace, I have not found it anywhere. India, our very own Bharathabhoomi, is the place where answers for all complex questions can be found, remedies for all spiritual aches. That's why I came back here. We Indians are good at deceiving foreigners by the mere mention of words such as Aathma, Brahmam, the Great Bliss, Kundalini and so on. There are as many fools abroad as there are in our country—perhaps even more. Here's the problem though: if there is a thing called conscience inside us, at some point it will start niggling us, asking, "Why do you con these hapless creatures?" I decided to give it all up when I couldn't deal with the pressure of that question any more, and decided to attain self-awareness by submitting myself to the tutelage of a woman. She's not as worldly-wise as I am, but she knows much more than I do about the common man's spiritual and material pain. I have come here looking for that woman.'

'Swami, where are you going now?'

'This woman, Jalajadevi, lives here in Kuliyanmukku. She possesses a secret mantra, one that will soothe the distress in my soul and elevate my spirit to the purest and loftiest form of bliss. A naadi jyotishi in Thanjavur who read my horoscope told me about her. I am going to see Devi. Would you like to come with me?'

'Of course. I'll follow you anywhere, jungle or desert.'

And off I went with that expectant, truth-seeking gentleman.

Devi's ashram was around fourteen kilometres away from town. We took a taxi. Although he'd said that this was his first trip, my guru seemed to know the way there and gave precise directions to the taxi driver saying, 'Turn left here,' and, 'Take the cut-road next to that big building,' and, 'Turn right,' and so on. Eventually, we reached Devi's ashram. Well, not so much of an ashram but more of a house. 'House' seemed a more appropriate name for that building which, despite being in the architectural style of a modern place of worship, looked neither affluent nor very clean.

Upon entering the yard, we were met by two pretty young women carrying silver trays on which lay Mysore plantains studded with sandalwood incense sticks. They bowed in unison and chimed, 'Welcome.'

With hearts brimming with joy, we followed these maidens inside, into a good-sized drawing room furnished with an exceptionally ugly sofa and a teapoy. The walls of the room looked as if a child had been let loose on them with some colours to draw elephants and boats and birds and flowers.

I sat there for over five minutes, looking at those pictures. The sound of a conch brought us to our feet. In another five minutes, Jalajadevi appeared, accompanied by a servant. She was dressed in a shimmering red silk sari with a sleeveless blouse, and wore a long garland of jasmine around her neck. She carried a rose in one hand and a gold-coloured—it may have even been solid gold—hatchet about six inches long in the other. On her head was a crown similar to those worn by goddesses in dance-dramas. Despite all these embellishments, the moment I laid eyes on her, I recognized her—I was absolutely certain that she was the same Jalaja who had been my classmate at the Polytechnic. I gave her a nice wide smile, and didn't bother to hide the fact that I had recognized her.

My guru, meanwhile, had prostrated himself at her feet and was wailing, calling her 'Amma' and 'Devi'. Jalaja gestured to him to get up.

'Don't fret,' she said to him. 'She'll come back. Just wait another three months. When you were here last time, did I not tell you it will take six months? And that was exactly three months ago. Your wife has started feeling the heat. You may not even have to wait the whole three months.'

Happiness spread across my guru's face like sunlight across the dawn sky. Now I was sure that this was not the first time he had met Jalajadevi. I couldn't figure out why he tried to make me believe otherwise.

'Have you sent your oldest child for coaching in Thrissur?' Jalajadevi asked.

'Yes, of course,' said my guru, with the utmost respect. He took out a bundle of thousand-rupee notes and placed it on the silver platter that the servant was holding. He then pointed to me and said, 'This is my disciple. Please bless him too.'

By then I had decided there was no point in continuing with this charade.

'Jalaja,' I said, 'did you not run away with driver Lalu half-way through the second year at Poly? So when did you . . .'

Before I could finish the sentence, two burly men—her security guards—rushed at me and, lifting me up bodily, ran out to the back of the house. Jalaja's house sat on a piece of land ten or twelve cents in area, surrounded by a man-high wall. When we reached the wall, the goons raised me above their heads and threw me over.

Respected readers, please do not involve yourself with a swami or a sanyasi or anyone dressed like one. Do not listen to their advice. Remember I told you about Gogol, right at the beginning of this diary? Do you know what happened to him toward the end of his life?

Gogol got involved with a spiritual guru by the name of Matvey Konstantinovsky. Konstantinovsky convinced Gogol that all his stories, novels and plays were sinful, and that he would be punished for his sins after his death. That poor writer! He was devastated, mentally and physically. One night, he set fire to the manuscript of the second part of his work, *Dead Souls*. He became bedridden soon after, and starved himself for nine days and died.

A pity, what else could one say? If Gogol had not been caught up in Konstantinovsky's clutches, none of this would have happened to him. There is one other shocking episode in this saga. Gogol's body was moved from its original burial site to another cemetery. When they opened up his coffin for this purpose, his body was found to be lying face down. There could be only one explanation: that he turned over in his coffin—in his grave. Meaning that he was buried before he was actually dead. You see . . . What an astonishing and miserable end to a great writer who was venerated by the likes of Dostoevsky and Mikhail Bulgakov.

My blood boiled, remembering these terrible things that happened to such a great writer. I began shouting abuses at my guru—indeed, at all spiritual gurus. Calling them feckless imbeciles and con artists incapable of suggesting rational practical solutions to even the simplest of a man's problems in life, I ran around the perimeter of Jalaja's house. I must have been on my fourth or fifth lap when a police jeep arrived. Two policemen jumped out and dragged me into the jeep.

At the police station, I was soundly beaten by the sub-inspector and by the policemen. I felt that the SI would have liked to detain me for a couple more days and continued working me over. But—someone somewhere must have called and intervened—I was taken to the magistrate's house by evening. He remanded me into custody for fourteen days, and I was taken to the sub-jail.

At the jail, the warders also gave me a proper thrashing. Unlike the policemen, their beatings were accompanied by vulgar and insinuating comments about me and Jalaja—'Did the sight of her make you horny,' and so on.

I was detained there for forty-seven days. My jail life was not particularly eventful. The worst experience was having to sleep on a rug on the floor with twelve others, in a room big enough only for five. Oh, human beings are of many hues.

There are those who get into pointless political quarrels just to annoy people, and others who, under the illusion of being gifted musicians, sing in horrible voices. Then there are the ones who speak terrible vulgarities, release thunderous farts in the middle of the night, moan in the ecstasy of sexual dreams. The worst are those who are addicted to drugs and alcohol. After a couple of days inside, their bodies and minds undergo such indescribable changes from withdrawal. Some are completely blind to everything and everyone in front of them. They pretend not to see the person lying asleep on the floor and trample over them. Even the beatings don't seem to affect them, except for the groans of immediate pain. But the strangest of all were the two people I met who, like proper madmen, walked around in circles, drawing pictures in the air. Almost all of these people seemed to care nothing about food. Some would even sleep through for twenty-four hours.

There was one guy who would start whistling as soon as everyone lay down to sleep. Apparently, he regularly broke into CD shops and also had a small habit of smoking ganja. His whistling was bearable for about ten-fifteen minutes, after which people would start hollering, 'Stop, you pube,' and other such profanities, which would soon escalate into a proper shouting match. The warders would come running and take him away, and everything would be quiet for a while. Then the warders would carry him back to the room. They gave him a quite specialized kind of beating. He would be completely incapable of lifting his chest or arms, and would slide on to his mat groaning throughout the night. In the morning, when everyone was herded out for using toilets, he would still be asleep.

He wouldn't hear the warders asking, 'What Vinu, aren't you going to get up? Don't you want to whistle?' Sometimes his body would be burning up. I don't know how, but most times by noon the fever would have come down. For the next two days, he would look like a chicken with avian flu. In the time I spent there, this series of events happened to him at least three or four times. One time, the warders had to cart him off to the hospital because the fever wouldn't go down. In spite of all this, the moment he regained movement in his right arm and could lift his body up, he'd be back to his whistling in the night.

It was in jail that I realized what a difficult and rare thing love was. I felt that no one was capable of really loving another person. Even the people who pretended to be close to me behaved in that way. A lot of the people who were brought to the jail after me got bail and were released, but some of us—like me and Vinu—had to stay put. I was upset that, even though we had our differences, my brother-in-law did not try to post bail for me. It really made me depressed. The only people who came to see me in jail were Barfly Pappan and Sukesan. I am not under any illusion that Pappan cares for me. In fact, I've never felt that he cared for anyone. Pappan's methodology was to bum five or ten rupees off even the most casual of acquaintances, and as soon as he had enough for a couple of pegs he'd run to the bar. A couple of hours later, he'd be scrounging off people all over again. Would someone like him ever be able to care for anything other than alcohol? Would he be able to love anyone wholeheartedly? And yet, Pappan came to see me, and even gave me thirty rupees.

Sukesan's situation is even worse than Pappan's. His routine is to sit in Karunettan's chai shop and find fault with the world at large. Communism—no good; capitalism—no good; parliamentary democracy—no good. This is no good; that is no good. He gets his kicks out of arguing against anything that the majority supports. And if anyone thinks of winning a debate with him, that person will definitely go mad. The man never tires of talking. Karunettan says that he has all this energy because he is unmarried.

Sukesan has no family except for his mother. She does cleaning jobs in a few houses. He sponges off her, stealing from the little money she makes to support his tea-and-cigarette habit, which fuels his energy for finding fault with the entire world. Even this Sukesan came to see me. He told me that the idea of prison itself was antisocial. A chap named Foucault had said so, apparently. If it were entirely unavoidable, people could be put in open jails. He raged that those who ruled the country were more criminal than most of the criminals in prisons, and that the police and the army were merely their servants. To top it all, he said all of this within earshot of the superintendent and the head warder.

Anyway . . . Jail life was suffocating in many ways. I was not beaten after the first couple of days. Still . . . Every couple of days, one of the warders would taunt me in front of everyone: 'What, my friend, shouldn't you be thinking about going to see Jalajadevi? You can't just hang around here having fun.'

There were many such painful incidents; no point in rehashing all of that. But let me tell you about the only pleasant experience I had during my time in jail. Within a couple of weeks of my incarceration, the superintendent and the head clerk took a liking to me. And so I became—you could say they made me—like a peon there. Sweeping the super's room and the jail veranda, providing the warders with mud pots of boiled and cooled water to drink, taking messages from the warders to fellow prisoners, preparing buttermilk for visiting lawyers, ward members or the super's friends, the writer and the teacher—all these became my duties. Actually, I was being humble when I said I was like a peon. I was really more like a messiri, an overseer. The warders even called me 'Messiri'.

One day, a Kuravan was brought in as a remand prisoner. His name was Lakshmanan. He was accused of nicking a mobile phone from a fellow in the crowd that had assembled to watch him perform with his monkey in the town market. They brought his monkey along to the jail too, and tethered it to a small mango tree within sight of the super's room. The monkey was also called Lakshmanan. Everyone called the Kuravan 'Lachanettan', and the monkey 'Lachanan'.

Lachanettan was a great entertainer. People made him tell stories late into the night. All his stories were about his exploits with women. He must have been around fifty years old, and he claimed to have had relations with ninety women. He would go into great detail about the physical and mental prowess of each woman he had sex with, describing each sexual act in great detail. Shafi, who was arrested for visa fraud, said one day:

'Lachanetta, you were not born to go around with a dancing monkey. You are a great man meant to gain fame as a successful writer.'

'Shafi, my man, you are spot on,' Lachanettan replied. 'Unfortunately, I am illiterate. It's too late now to start learning. This is my life. What to do, this is what is written on my head. Shaving my head is not going to erase what's already been written there.' Lachanettan's voice shook with unshed tears.

The head warder and others stayed up until ten or eleven

in the night, playing cards. Card-playing, obviously, has to be accompanied by alcohol consumption. One night, during this drinking session, the head warder poured some brandy in a paper glass and gave it to Lachanettan's monkey. That became a regular thing, and now the monkey Lachanan had to have a couple of pegs every night. I was not aware of this development.

One day, I went out to sweep around the mango tree where Lachanan was tethered. To my misfortune, I had a paper glass in my hand. As soon as he saw it, he jumped up in front of me and began making a strange noise. Taken by surprise, I was utterly frightened and scrambled back, dropping the paper glass. Lachanan must have thought that there was some brandy or rum for him in it. He jumped on top of me in anger, and gave two resounding slaps on each of my cheeks. I have no idea how I managed to jump back and escape without being assaulted further. I have no doubt he would have scratched my face to shreds otherwise.

When I told the head warder what had happened, he and all the others roared with laughter.

Anyway, the very next day, Lachanettan was released on bail. But the monkey Lachanan seemed reluctant to leave. Lachanettan untied the rope from the mango tree and called to him, 'Come on, Lachanan, get moving.' Lachanan raised his hands to his head as if to say, 'O my Lord, what a misfortune.' He rolled on the ground, screeching loudly and looking at the warders miserably as if begging them to rescue him. Every time Lachanettan tried to pull him forward, Lachanan pulled himself backward. But how long could the poor thing resist? An angry and merciless Lachanettan finally managed to drag him out of the prison. And off they went.

20 November, Tuesday

I have been suffering from a cough and congestion for the last
five to ten days. Finally, the day before yesterday, I went to see
Dr P.G.P. Pothuval, the chest specialist at Sulabha Memorial
Hospital. This famous physician is an octogenarian. Apparently,
once upon a time, he was number-one among the eminent doctors at the medical college. After retirement, in addition to treat-
ing people, he has been proving his eminence in the real estate
business and spare-parts trade. Dr Pothuval was one of those
people who turned everything they touched into gold. It is said
that, despite his advanced years, he was an expert in identify-
ing TB, asthma, allergies, cancer and any other disease relating
to the respiratory system as soon as he laid eyes on the patient.
Although he charged an enormous fee—unheard of, in these
parts—his consultation rooms were always crowded. I was able
to see him on a Saturday, only because I went straight to the
hospital on the previous Wednesday morning at eight o'clock
and booked an appointment. The token number I got was thirteen. I lost all hope as soon as I saw that number, but I couldn't
afford to postpone seeing the doctor to another day for a more
auspicious token number. So I decided to go on Saturday. It
must have been the high demand, the doctor was seeing two or
three patients at the same time. It was only when I went in and
watched it myself that I got a sense of how this setup worked.

There were two nurses in the room. When I went in, one
of them was writing a number on the forearm of a man who
had taken off his shirt and mundu and was sitting on a stool
in the corner. I reckoned that was preparation for allergy test-
ing. On the stool in front of the doctor sat another scrawny

man. A third one was lying on the examination table behind him. While examining this man with his stethoscope, the doctor gestured to the man in front of him to extend his tongue. And in between all this, he talked to the nurse who was taking my blood pressure:

'Has Jayamohan arrived, Sister?'

The nurse nodded. As she wrote down my blood pressure on a prescription pad, he asked:

'When did he arrive?'

'Yesterday. After twelve o'clock.'

'Oh, that must be why you're looking so tired,' he said, with a sleazy smile.

An expression that combined happiness, shyness and displeasure appeared for a split second on the nurse's face. She poked the tip of her tongue out and subtly contorted her features, and went to the door to call in the next patient.

The nurse doing the allergy test shook with laughter.

The patient who was lying on the examination table got up. The doctor asked him to sit on the chair in front of him, and turned to the patient on the stool:

'You're still smoking, aren't you?'

'No, sir.'

'Don't lie to me.'

'No, sir,' he repeated. But the doctor had stopped paying attention to him, and addressed the patient on the chair:

'I've made a slight change in your medication. You can't get it in the store here. When you go out, look for the green-painted shop on the right. They'll have it. Come back after one month.'

As soon as he got up, the patient on the stool moved to

the chair, and the nurse gestured to me to sit on the stool. I was about to sit down, when the doctor asked me to lie down on the examination table. Then he said to the patient on the chair:

'I'll write some medicine for you this one last time. Do not step into this room again if you can't give up smoking.'

The nurse had already brought in the next patient and was taking his blood pressure.

The doctor didn't ask me anything about my illness. He placed the stethoscope on my chest, asked me to inhale and exhale, and said:

'You need an X-ray. Come back with it as soon as you can.'

As I left, taking the doctor's note with me, the nurse came after me and said: 'Come back within half an hour. The doctor will leave early today.'

Luckily, there was not much of a crowd at the X-ray room.

By the time I got back to the doctor's room, the allergy-test guy had finished his test and was sitting in front of the doctor, fully dressed. The doctor looked at the test results and laughed loudly:

'You seem to be allergic to everything except chicken. You're even allergic to rice! Well, we can't give you any medicine for allergies then. I'm prescribing another medicine for two weeks. You won't find it in the store here. Buy it from Jenny Medicals near the bus stand.'

Now there was a seriously obese man and an average-sized man sitting on two chairs in front of the doctor. Without even glancing my way, the doctor asked them:

'So, what seems to be the trouble?'

Average Guy patted Fat Guy's shoulder and said, 'We need to get his weight reduced, Doctor. It is a great inconvenience to him.'

'Which idiot advised them to come to me with this request?' the doctor seemed to be wondering. His expression betrayed his puzzlement for a split second and, seeing it, I felt a little smile escape me. The doctor may have noticed it; he suddenly turned all business-like.

'What's your weight?' the doctor asked in a gruff voice.

'180 kilos,' Fat Guy stroked his Bulganin beard and replied in an offhand voice. He seemed to have forgotten that he had come here to find a solution to his problem.

But the doctor didn't seem to care. 'Where are you working?'

'I'm in Dubai.'

'And what work do you do?'

'I'm in business.'

'Do you suffer from congestion?'

'Sometimes.'

'Okay.' He turned to the nurse who had poked her tongue at him earlier. 'How about giving him an allergy test, Sister?'

The nurse replied with a teasing smile, 'Of course, Doctor. Why not?'

'Okay, then. Go and get an X-ray done first,' the doctor said to Fat Guy.

As they got up, the doctor asked for my X-ray film and looked at it. That's when I realized that he could barely see.

'There is nothing wrong here. You have a bit of congestion. I'll prescribe a medicine. Take it and come back after ten days.'

'It's not available in the store here, is it?' I asked.

I think the doctor did not expect such a response, and he totally lost it:

'Who the hell are you to decide that? In that case, why don't you write your own prescription?'

He threw the prescription pad in front of me. The doctor's voice and expression seemed to scare the two nurses and a patient who was already in the room. I, on the other hand, felt no fear at all. Without speaking, I pushed the prescription pad back toward him. My facial expression may have scared him, because he took the prescription pad and, obediently, as if doing a gravely responsible job, wrote down the medicines. As I got up to leave, I said, 'For the time being, I don't need the allergy test, do I doctor?'

So that's today, over and done with. It must be the syrup to relieve the congestion, I am feeling extremely sleepy.

23 November, Friday

This evening, I saw the eighty-three-year-old man whom everyone respectfully and lovingly calls 'Uchilettan' coming out of Baalika Sadanam, the home for girls, looking very worried. He seemed to be in a great hurry and in greater consternation.

'Uchiletta, what brings you here?' I asked.

'You know, a girl from our village has been brought here. I came here to threaten her.'

'Which girl? Why would you want to threaten a girl?'

'You know, the girl who was in class four at Kizhakkekara school. She was raped in broad daylight by her father and some other fellows day before yesterday.'

'And . . . ?'

'She is still a naïve little thing, isn't she? If she starts blath-
ering to the police, the shame of it is on all of us local people.'

Uchilettan didn't wait for my reply. He took off as fast as
he could, limping and swaying, as if to escape from something.

Honestly, I still haven't understood what the issue really
was.

Why did Uchilettan feel that he had to preserve the honour of his kinsmen and threaten this little nine-year-old girl
who was raped by her own father and relatives? Did someone
give him this task? Or did he give himself the responsibility?

I have tried really hard to believe that everything I saw and
heard today was the product of my imagination. But how could
I have conjured up Uchilettan, whom I saw in the flesh, from
my imagination? The words he rasped out are still ringing in my
ears. And I can see, as if still in front of my eyes, the dilapidated
building among the dusty trees, with the faded sign 'Baalika
Sadanam' hanging in front of it.

25 November, Sunday

I spent all evening at the beach. It was crowded as it was Sunday.
People were enjoying themselves—driving along the beach,
swimming in the sea, strolling in the sea breeze, laughing and
flirting with each other. I used to feel somewhat put off, watching people enjoying themselves doing these things. But not any
more. Whether it is me, you or anyone else, we only have one
life. So enjoy it to the fullest, that's all there is to it. Me, though,
forget about enjoying to the fullest, I barely have the financial
means to stand up straight.

Depending on Amma for money has become a matter of
considerable shame. As for finding a job—I can't decide what

job to do. I can do house painting, electrification, repairs. But those are jobs that people recognize as 'jobs'. I don't want those kinds of jobs. What I have in mind is the job of a political leader, or a minister, member of parliament, professor, businessman, etc. I can do any of these jobs, but so far no one has invited me to do any of these. If someone made me the prime minister, I would have shown exactly how to rule this country. I sat on a cement bench among the casuarina trees, thinking deeply about this, and fell asleep inadvertently. When I woke up, the beach was filled with moonlight. There was not a single soul in the visible distance, and the sea was roaring loudly. I don't know why, but I suddenly felt very frightened. Walking alone on a deserted, moonlit beach is a terrible experience. Usually, the sand on the beach is easy to walk on, but tonight, every step felt as if I had to pull my foot out of the sand with some difficulty. I was soaked in sweat despite the strong sea breeze. Hunger, thirst and fear assaulted me together.

I dragged myself forward, foot by foot, feeling upset that if it wasn't for the accursed moment when I fell asleep on the bench, I'd have been home by now. All of a sudden, a strange being appeared before me. He was so tall that he appeared to be touching the sky. He had a human-like face, a body covered in scales, and a phallus and testicles that seemed to be made of bronze. The scales were not scary or horrifying. Instead, they were beautifully coloured, as if created by a gifted artist, and exuded a pleasing fragrance.

'Why are you here so late?' the being asked me in an ancient voice.

'I fell asleep.'

'Do you know who I am?'

'No.'

'I am the Old Man of the Sea. There are over a hundred of us in different seas. We are not a literary metaphor, as you had assumed so far.'

'What kind of work do your people do?'

'We don't have any particular work as such. We can live as long as we want, and die whenever we please without any trouble. We can eat whatever we want from the sea, travel wherever we please on the backs of sea turtles, whales or dolphins. Nobody controls or scolds us. Recently, though, there's been an explosion in ocean traffic, and there are some difficulties because of that. But we are invisible to the human eye and none of their scopes can find us. There are beautiful palaces under the sea for us to live in, where we can frolic with sea nymphs to our hearts' content.'

God, what a life! No work, and all play and pleasure. Nobody on earth—not even a minister or MP or political leader or business tycoon—could achieve that.

Perhaps I could also have such a life, if this Old Man of the Sea were to be so kind. I resolved to form a strong, lasting friendship with him. But just as I was about to start a sweetly-worded conversation with him, he stepped right back into the sea and walked swiftly away across the waves.

'Hey, hey,' I called out and ran after him. I had taken five or six steps into the sea, when a roaring wave crashed over me and I was submerged.

I suppose it was not my time to die yet. There were two policemen on the beach, and they jumped in to rescue me. One of them got a hold on my arm and, together, they pulled me out and deposited me on the beach. They were on duty here, following complaints from the locals about antisocial activities at night.

I thought the policemen who saved my life would take me home on their bike or jeep. Instead, they fetched their lathi from their tent and started beating me, shouting, 'Run, you son of a bitch, get lost. Jumping into the sea in the middle of the night, making work for the rest of us...' I cried as loudly as I could, vainly hoping that the Old Man of the Sea would hear me and come to my rescue, blowing away the policemen like milkweed seeds.

The policemen conducted their assault in an entirely scientific manner. They beat me only below my knees. Even then, my legs should have been injured beyond repair. But there was not a single welt or scratch to be seen, and not even a shred of pain remained. So what did happen? Did I imagine all that? Did I not even go to the beach? Did I make it all up in my mind like a fantastic story?

27 November, Tuesday

Amma has been suffering from a terrible headache since morning. She didn't even make me a cup of tea, but gave me a thorough scolding instead. She gets these headaches once every two or three months, and when it comes she gets exceptionally angry. I was truly dejected by the scolding I received as soon as I woke up in the morning.

I went out at around 11 AM The first person I saw on the road was the lottery ticket vendor, Dasettan. This poor soul has been selling lottery tickets for a long time. I've heard of people who had won five or ten thousand rupees. I've also heard of one fellow who bought a ticket for ten rupees and won twenty rupees. But poor Dasettan had not won anything so far.

'Come on, Aagi, buy a ticket. It's the Christmas bumper, only one hundred rupees, but you could win a crore,' Dasettan said.

It was his lucky day as I had a hundred-rupee note and another thirty-five rupees with me. I got it from *Oru Desathinte Katha* by S.K. Pottekkatt that I had borrowed from Gandhi Smaraka Library yesterday—a windfall, thanks to the forgetfulness of some respected reader who likes to store his money in books. It is the end of the month, so there is no great harm in me spending this money. When Amma receives her pension and I get my spending money, I could put it back and return the book. There is no doubt that books are a person's closest relatives.

I felt sure of one thing as I handed over the hundred-rupee note and bought the ticket from Dasettan—I would win the lottery this time. I didn't have to think too long about what to do if I did win, because I had an idea immediately: I would buy some fertile land here and in Wayanad and Idukki, and start farming brahmi. There is no better thing than brahmi to sharpen the intellect and increase memory power.

People, generally, are losing both intellectual prowess and memory power. So brahmi farmers would conquer the world in the future, and I would be one among them.

There are a lot of things that can be farmed in this world. So why did I think of brahmi first? The answer came to me immediately: When I was in school, my nickname was Brahmigoyindan. The term 'brahmi' was added to my name when I was in class seven. I had a girlfriend in those days. Well, I am calling her my 'girlfriend' in hindsight—we had no idea what that meant in those days. Anyway, I really liked her. I would go and stand in front of class six-B in the morning, at noon and during intervals, just to catch a glimpse of her. I couldn't get my fill of seeing her or thinking about her. I wanted to give her something special and, after much deliberation, I pulled up a few brahmi plants from the side of the fields near my house, put them in a plastic bag, gave it to her and said:

'Grind these up in milk and drink. It's very good for memory power. You'll get good marks in maths.'

By this time, my throat was completely dry and I was drenched in sweat.

Kanakalatha—that was her name—took the brahmi straight to my class teacher, along with a complete recap of my dialogue. My class teacher was someone who took great pleasure in catching and punishing even the mildest of infractions across sexes. 'So you like giving brahmi to girls and increasing their memory power, do you?' He made fun of me and boxed my ears in front of everyone. He didn't stop there—he took me to the headmaster. The headmaster was a terrifying person who was known as 'Othenan of the Cane' out of respect for his propensity to wield the cane as expertly as Othenan—the martial arts hero from northern Kerala—wielded the urumi, his trademark long-sword. He delivered a few burning lashes on the inside of my palm as if I had committed a great sin, saying: 'Get lost, Brahmi, you're not even fully hatched yet. Don't let me ever catch you even glancing at girls again.'

And that's how I became Brahmigoyindan. How I came to acquire the moniker 'Goyindan' along with Brahmi instead of my real name is something I can't recall now. I lost both nicknames after I left school.

Anyway, I was telling you about my plans for farming brahmi. My brahmi farm would extend to the horizon, and I would stroll through it in the early morning mist and the moonlight at night. I would go to Kochi twice a month to see off brahmi exports to foreign parts. The owners of big American and Australian medical companies would come looking for me. I would write a book titled *Brahmi and Brahma* and newspapers would publish an article about me titled something like 'The Lord of the Intellect'. I'd be interviewed on TV, and good-looking mothers who spend large amounts of money to educate their children in expensive schools would come to see me. Gently swaying on my swing, I would converse with them about brahmi.

All through the day, thoughts about brahmi overtook my mind, and I found myself not being able to focus on anything else. It was all I could think about—on the bus, in the chai shop, on my aimless walks . . . *Sarvam brahmimayam*. All that was, was brahmi. Try as I might, I could not get brahmi out of my mind. Slowly, my enthusiasm for brahmi farming started to wane and, by evening, I began to feel very scared. Perhaps this was how brahmi insinuated itself into one's intellect and started taking over, I began to fear.

On the journey home that night, the bus was so crowded that it was difficult to even breathe. As I stood, crushed and stamped upon by strangers, my thoughts about brahmi continued to soar. By then, I was overwhelmed with fear that I was losing my sanity, and my insides cried out.

It was when I got home and took off my shirt to hang it on the hook that my mind started cooling down, as if from a sudden downpour in the midst of a scorching summer. The lottery ticket I had bought was not in my shirt pocket. In the crowded bus, someone had picked my pocket and saved my life.

30 November, Friday

I don't think these days anyone really believes that only the diaries of dignitaries and celebrities are worth publishing. Personally, I have no doubt at all about this matter, and I would like to see this diary published as soon as possible. So, as soon as I finish today's entry, I will send it for publication without further ado.

Like most writers these days, I too think that this is a number-one work of literature. But, there is one difference, and it is that I couldn't give a toss if any of you readers say that this diary is a load of crap. And that is because I am a madman.

Anyone can say whatever they want about me, find pleasure in bad-mouthing me. It will not affect me. Have you heard of a Chinese philosopher called Lao Tzu? I heard about him recently. He lived in the sixth century BC. For a couple of months, I took him on as my spiritual guru. That's how I am—I don't have a permanent guru. My first guru was Sri Buddha; then it was Confucius. After that it was Padinjare Veetil Govindettan, followed by Lao Tzu. Then came Naxal Usman, a.k.a. Alummukku Usman. Is there anyone we cannot learn from? Confucius cannot teach what Govindettan can. Anyway, getting back to Lao Tzu who said: 'No one can dishonour me because I don't need anyone to honour me.' This is my attitude too. You can try all you want, but you will not be able to dishonour me. Let that be.

Yesterday afternoon, a rooster came into our yard. As soon as I saw him, I felt a great respect for him. Good posture, good looks and good intellect. He asked me, 'What's up? What's happening in politics these days?'

'Nothing much. The leaders continue with their pilfering, and the followers call out "Zindabad" and get all worked up and emotional. That's all.'

'No new formations of counter-powers?'

'No. Nothing seems to be taking shape. Oh, there are many existing problems—fear, intense self-love, lack of munificence, various philosophical nostalgias, stubbornness, tantrums, general incapacities, and so on and so forth.'

'I've been noticing these things too. There is not even a dim ray of light on the horizon.' He continued with great sadness, 'I am leaving.'

'Where are you going?'

'To the deep jungle.'

'How will you live there?'

'I am not going there to live. I am going there to die. It will only be a matter of five or ten minutes before someone will end my life in the forest.'

I didn't reply. I accompanied this brave soul who was leaving to seek his death up to the chain fence put up by forestry officials, and came back struggling to control my tears.

I went home, had my lunch and slept for over four hours. After that, I left home deciding to walk the three kilometres into town. The first thing you see when you get into town is the children's park. I was intrigued to find a small crowd in front of it, so I went to check it out and saw something there that was completely unexpected. My jail-mate Lachanettan was there with his monkey, entertaining the crowd. By the time I got there, the show was almost over. People threw one-, two- and five-rupee coins on the cloth spread in front of Lachanettan, and as he gathered them up and straightened his back, he saw me.

'Hello Bhai!' As soon as he called out to me, his monkey, Lachanan, also recognized me. I'd only heard about the pure excitement and ecstasy that true love can bring. I saw it for the first time today in the monkey Lachanan, as he came running and fell at my feet, almost as if asking for forgiveness for slapping me in the face a while back. He then jumped up on me and, before I could do anything, sat on my shoulder.

'Bhai, my Lachanan is very smart,' Lachanettan said. 'I've to go for a dongals nearby. I'll be back in half an hour. Let him stay with you until then.' He walked away before I could reply. 'Dongals' was Lachanettan's preferred term for a sexual liaison.

I stood outside the park with Lachanan. Half an hour became one hour, then two, three ... The hours went by. By nine o'clock, I couldn't bear the insult and the sadness. Frightening thoughts began to form in my mind. Was Lachanettan caught while engaging in dongals? Did someone capture him and tie him up on a coconut tree? Or did the morality police catch hold of him and beat him to death? This monkey with me was a wild animal. I wasn't sure which legal category he belonged to. I don't think anyone would file a legal case if they saw a Kuravan with a monkey, but I knew for a fact that there'd be consequences if I were to go around with a monkey—perhaps even a police case. And it was an absolute certainty that if I were to end up in jail again, no one would come to bail me out.

I racked my brain, but could not come up with a plan on what to do with Lachanan. Finally, I decided to take him home. As expected, this decision created an almighty palaver.

Amma made a scene, beating her chest and crying loudly. My neighbours came running, hearing the ruckus. Recalling some long-ago experience of monkey entertainment, they tried to engage Lachanan:

'How does the bride stand beside her bridegroom, Rama . . . ?'

'Show us how Sita sat in Ravanan's Lanka, Rama . . .'

Lachanan ignored them. He mimicked drinking, as if asking for a glass of brandy or rum, and licked his lips urgently. And when he saw that the assembled people did not understand what he was trying to convey, he became aggressive and began displaying his teeth and shaking his bum at them. Seeing this, some children started throwing stones at him, and Lachanan shrieked and lunged at them. When the laughter, whistles and general mayhem became unbearable, I shouted at all of them and sent them on their way.

When they all left, I gave Lachanan a few biscuits, a banana and a bottle of water. Then, attaching a long piece of rope to the chain already around his neck, I tethered him to a jackfruit tree. If a dog or a fox came in the night, he would be able to climb up the tree and be safe. As I was walking away, Lachanan caught my leg, and when I turned and looked at him, he stood on his hind legs and gestured to me to face him. I lowered my face to his and Lachanan stroked my cheeks as if to soothe me. An expression came upon his face as if to say, 'This poor human. What difficulties he had to put up with because of me . . .' His eyes began watering and, feeling an overwhelming emotion in the presence of such love, I cried too, holding him close to my chest.

It's after one o'clock in the night now. The cold air outside is slowly crawling into this room. I have no more mental strength to think or to do anything. I am going to stop writing this diary for now. I don't know what happened to Lachanettan, nor can I imagine what to do with Lachanan. There is no saying what will happen tomorrow. That's life, isn't it? Let it happen as it happens. Let me stop. Thank you. Goodbye.

Oru Malayali Bhranthante Diary, 2013

N. Prabhakaran
In conversation with Jayasree Kalathil

N. Prabhakaran in conversation with Jayasree Kalathil

DHARMADAM, 12 JUNE 2018

JK: The first story of yours that I translated was 'Oru Malayali Bhranthante Diary' (Diary of a Malayali Madman). I have a particular fascination for works that disturb or even disrupt the idea of a shared 'consensus reality', as well as works where those people who are able to traverse this boundary get to tell their stories. The stories we have selected for this collection all have this theme in common. They made sense to me because the stories are about people who are usually called 'abnormal'. But looking at it another way, they are all about people who have the ability to access what I like to call 'non-consensual reality'. These are real worlds, dream worlds, as well as surreal worlds. Your work has always represented these other possible worlds as seen through the eyes of ordinary, everyday people. I am thinking about 'Ottayante Paappan' (Mahout of a Rogue Tusker) for which you won the Mathrubhumi Prize for short stories by college students in 1971.

NP: I am fascinated by the possibility of these different worlds. Definitely, 'Ottayante Paappan' is one of the stories in which I have explored this. The protagonist in that story is someone who struggles with a kind of disconnect in his psyche as well as in his thinking; someone who is caught up in empathy for the oppressed and anger against social wrongs, while also compelled to maintain a safe distance from it all. I had no knowledge of psychology then, and didn't write the story consciously thinking about this psychic tug-of-war and what the distress experienced as a result of it might be like. Reviewing the story, a prominent literary critic of the day wrote in a sympathetic tone, but I think also with a tinge of mockery, that this youngster – I was only eighteen then – is in the hands of the Existentialists. The fact is that in those days I had no knowledge of Existentialism. I was not writing in the line of Existentialists. I simply felt that the conventional beliefs, parameters of value judgements and several practices a society tightly holds are diametrically opposite to the ideas, feelings and sentiments an individual nurses in their inner self. This contradiction inevitably leads to a tragic end.

A few years ago, I had a near-fatal accident. It seems to have affected my confidence in many ways. For instance, I find myself somewhat scared when I have to tackle a flight of steps. I also had some serious problems with my lungs recently. All of this seems to have caused several limitations to my movement, and my public life has been curtailed to a large extent. At the same time, I find that, on the mental plain, I feel a kind of freedom or unboundedness, and I sense that it is beginning to reflect in my writing. I have almost completely given up on ideological editing of my writing now. Even before the accident I would try to write freely, but there would always be something that asserted itself somewhat pedagogically. Now I am able to let go. 'Tender Coconut' is one of the stories written after the accident and it is written exactly as it came to me.

Nowadays, the seed of a plot that falls into my mind sprouts with a form without waiting for my consent, growing and branching up to magical skies. The sense of reality that we preserve within the boundaries of unchangeable, stable things that we call socially approved norms, customs, formalities and the like are least allowed to affect its growth.

JK: There are several depictions of 'madmen' in Malayalam fiction. But instances where they become protagonists with the freedom to tell their story from their point of view are few and far between. Our Malayali madman, Aagi, takes his task as a diarist very seriously. He is not just narrating his story but engaging socially within his milieu and recording it. How did you come about creating Aagi and the story?

NP: In fact, that story came about from the story of a monkey that a friend of mine, Rajesh, told me. Rajesh served as a jail warder in Kozhikode, Kasaragod and Thalassery sub-jails, and as the Deputy Prison Officer at Kannur Central Jail. Rajesh was my student at Government Brennen College and, after the college days, one of my closest friends. When he was working at the Thalassery sub-jail, we used to meet up in town regularly. On one such occasion, he told me about a prisoner who was charged with some petty crime and brought to the jail. This man had a monkey he took around markets and public places, making it perform, and that's how he earned his living. This monkey was also brought to the jail with him. The prison officers would feed this monkey and share their drinks with it and, by the time the prisoner was released, the monkey had become quite close to the prison officers. Ironically, the prison had become a place of freedom for the monkey now that he didn't have to perform for his owner or be ill-treated. When the man left, the monkey refused to leave and put up a fight until he was dragged away by his owner.

Rajesh had many such stories, and I would encourage him to write about them. Eventually, he wrote the book *Azhikalkkappuram (Ippuravum) – Inside the Bars (Also Outside)* – which was published posthumously. Rajesh died of cancer on 19 January 2017. The book contains excellent narratives of Rajesh's relationship with the prisoners. Anyway, it is through the many stories he told me about the prison and its inmates, especially about the monkey, that I got the first seeds for the plot.

The story is also a commentary on contemporary Kerala. Kerala is progressive and developed but, looking at it from a different angle, there is also something somewhat 'mad' about how we go about our politics, the grandiose nature of it all. You'll remember Aagi's commentaries on the politicians in his diary. The social life here has lost the charm of humaneness to a large extent. Here and there you may find people in all walks of life living with some principles. But there is widespread decay and despair. Offices function in the silently approved culture of red tape. Cultural activities have lost their vigour and become ritualistic. The first consideration of any organizer who plans a public programme is that it should in no way create displeasure for the authorities or the major political party of the area. Everybody is jubilantly eloquent about freedom of expression but, at the same time, is willing to join hands with hegemonic powers to silence anyone who presents their opinions and emotions without fear. As the revolutionary spirit has turned into a feeble shadow, all superstitions once driven out have come back to the centre stage of day-to-day life in Kerala. Nothing seems to be real – there is a level of deceit in it all. So we have to constantly ask questions about how 'normal' people are and how 'real' things are.

JK: In a sense, we have to ask questions about the idea of normality and reality itself.

NP: Yes, and the reflection of that in many areas of our lives.

JK: This is a running theme in the stories in this collection. You explore the cultural construction of what is deemed normal through what one might call everyday madness, especially in relation to politics, spirituality and spiritual life.

NP: I have always thought that many of the things that have social approval, things that are considered normal, are really what should be considered abnormal or even mad. I believe that, just like politics, the area of spirituality functions as a way to fool people while, internally, the people of Kerala generally experience a terrible sense of emptiness. I truly believe this. We have so many positive things in our society: for example, daily labourers are paid a better wage compared to many other parts of India; our government employees are also paid much better. We could say that people's lives as a whole are much smoother than before. But we have lost many things: ideological vigour, love for drama and other performing arts, interest in serious discussions about literature, philosophy, and the like. As individuals, we have become terribly anaemic in our social concerns, and as communicators we are perhaps the poorest. I would even say that we live in a state of broken-down communication and, as a result, are engulfed in a sense of emptiness. One might even ask: What is madness if not the inability to communicate?

In Kerala, politics works almost like caste: If your father was/is a Marxist, then you are a Marxist. If your father was/is a BJP supporter, then you are a supporter or activist for the BJP. That's how it works. Marxists, socialists and Gandhians are all totally apathetic in learning the political philosophy which is supposed to make them what they are. There is very little critical thinking involved in this. On an everyday level, people simply don't engage in any kind of critical reflection about the parties they support, functioning, instead, under a sense of obedience – a kind of caste-loyalty and duty to 'their' people. Beyond that, there is very little communication. It is difficult to imagine an alternative way of being, to get really involved in society, influence its thinking in any fundamental way.

JK: The 'mad' people in your stories – Aagi, Sreekumar, Mohanan, Georgekutty, Krishna – are really the commentators and chroniclers of this madness. This idea of inhabiting other worlds simultaneously is something that runs through all of the stories in this anthology. In essence, a sense of aloneness, and a disconnect of the mind and intellect rather than of the body, which might allow some people to become more receptive to worlds outside of consensus reality or a normality that is accepted and validated by sociocultural norms. As a person whose experience of these 'non-consensus realities' was diagnosed as 'psychosis', I think one reason I was attracted to these stories was because you enable this different way of thinking without being pedagogic about it. And within this possibility of traversing the gossamer-thin walls of reality and normality, each of your characters retain their own individuality.

NP: Yes, for example, I think Sreekumar in 'Pigman' and his intense reaction to the situation he finds himself in is quite different from Aagi and the way he goes about facing the world around him. Within the sociopolitical milieu of Kerala, our communications have become formalized, based on half-truths intended to hoodwink rather than reveal. In another sense, the manifestation of madness, if we can call it that, is in the pointless political and religious arguments that have made Kerala politics what it is at present. My fictional 'madmen' have come from my thoughts about the contemporary sociopolitical and cultural situation in Kerala. But within their own individual contexts, their reactions and actions are also quite individual.

I'd also like to comment here on the education system in the state. There is a widespread feeling that some fundamental errors have crept into the system and made it hollow. Teaching of literature and the humanities has been marginalized, and even at the post-graduate level the meaning of education has become a thoughtless collection of information. Thus, on many levels, even the highly educated turn out to be illiterate. Contradictions like this also demand a thorough rethinking of normality.

JK: I want to ask you about the story 'Invisible Forests' now. It is, in some ways, a prequel to your novel *Theeyoor Rekhakal* (Theeyoor Records) which won the first award of the EMS Memorial Trust, Munnad, in 2005. In it, you tell the social history of a 'suicide village' – an idea that is also at the centre of 'Invisible Forests'. There's plenty of research that has linked Kerala with high suicide rates as well as high alcohol consumption. Did you write the story, and later the novel, as a direct response to these issues?

NP: Dharmadam, where I have been living for about four decades now, was, not so long ago, a village that had especially high suicide rates. The idea of a 'suicide village' may have come from that. But beyond rates of suicides, there are the sociopolitical contexts. As I have already said, there is the issue of genuine communication between people. The public sphere is haunted by sheer apathy. Political parties compete to excel each other in arguments, especially at a performative level in visual and print media. But people have become largely apolitical. I think there is a sense of not belonging that this creates, especially among the youth who are also simultaneously struggling to find employment or other contexts for social interaction. Many of them turn to alcohol. This is a particular problem in northern Kerala. There used to be enabling spaces for political, literary and cultural discussions – reading rooms, libraries, other community spaces. Now, with the exception of a handful, these are functioning only formally. I have personal memories dating fifty or so years back, where every village had people interested in and promoting literature and reading as part of everyday village life. Literacy levels were lower, but engagement and interest with creative modes of communication were higher.

Let me give you an example: When G. Sankarakurup received the first Jnanpith Award in 1965 for *Odakkuzhal*, there was a big controversy here. Did Malayalam literature really deserve a Jnanpith? Was there any Kerala writer who deserved this accolade? This was primarily following a comment made by the then president of the Kerala Sahitya Akademi. He allegedly said something about Malayali writers being 'mukkananji' (of very low stature). So out came the reply from the people: 'If our writers are mukkananji, then you are Chief Mukkananji.' I remember heated discussions in many villages debating whether or not *Odakkuzhal* was a work worthy of the award. I have clear memories of taking part in this discussion – I was a high-school student then – in my own village.

What I am trying to say by way of this example is that such an interest and engagement with literature was alive in the villages. And it was something that enabled and supported village life and sociocultural interactions and communications within it. I believe firmly that this mode of communication is all but dead. Around 300 crore rupees worth of books are sold in Kerala every year, supported by government grants as well as commercially organized book markets. Yet, the culture of reading as part of everyday life has not grown with this. If anything, it has withered away. Instead, reading literature has become utilitarian, as part of a process of assignments and exams in schools and colleges. I would even argue that, while young people might be reading as part of this process, they are illiterate in terms of literary culture and the enjoyment and reflection that go with it. Derrida, Deleuze, Guattari, Foucault, Badiou and others are common subjects of literary discussions here. But when a genuinely different work appears, it takes months to form an opinion. The readings pretending to be up-to-date on a theoretical level fail to reach the crux of the content.

And there is a parallel process of decline in engagement with political philosophy as well. There was a time when Marxism was probably the most discussed subject in Kerala. These days, there are very few who engage with Marxism as political philosophy. Even the so-called staunch Marxists are not interested in knowing the later developments and changes in Marxist philosophy. For them, it is unthinkable to admit that many findings and predictions in the foundational texts of Marxism have become obsolete, and a redefining of their political stance, taking into consideration the economic, cultural and political realities of the contemporary world, is inevitable. I strongly feel that people who consider Marxism a religious doctrine which can only be approached with utmost reverence can never have a meaningful understanding of it. Communists should have the intellectual honesty to admit that an unwillingness to continuously update Marxism in accordance with changes and developments in all spheres of human life will make people reactionary, even if they vehemently argue for the philosophy.

Malayali philosophy was based on literature. Our big ideas have come from poetry and literature – Sri Narayana Guru's poetry, for example. The decline in that cultural process has created a vacuum. What remains is a context in which sensitive individuals find it hard to thrive, and experience mental and emotional distress. My understanding is that, in most cases, what gets termed as 'hallucination' and 'delusion' – madness, if you will – is a way of coping in this context, an attempt to overcome this situation through imagined worlds that might seem strange to others. Even those who exhibit a thorough practical sense and a sort of cunning in life accumulate energy for maintaining such qualities away from the life of unbridled imagination or 'hallucination' they lead secretly.

JK: Kerala boasts of a high literacy rate. But this idea that you are talking about – engagement with literature and political philosophy as a mode of communication – is different from the idea of literacy.

NP: Yes. Recently, I had been involved in two endeavours here in Kannur. One is in Alakode where there is a Readers' Forum. What we did is start a 'Sahitya Patashala' – a school of letters of sorts, based in the community. I chose Alakode to start this effort because of a friend of mine, Benny Sebastian, who is a karate master. Benny was part of organizing an event to commemorate a South Indian karate grandmaster,

Ravindran, on the occasion of a thousand of his students becoming black-belts. They were releasing a souvenir at this function, and Benny invited me to do the honours. I have no connection with karate, but I went. I had prepared a few short remarks on literature and reading and, when I began to speak, I found the entire audience, hundreds of them, listening very keenly, receiving each and every word with utmost interest and enthusiasm. This was a revelation to me. As I was talking, the idea that the experience of literature is thoroughly communicable, even to those whom we generally do not count while considering the teaching of literature, flashed through my mind. Later, I thought very seriously about it. The possibility of training people in the appreciation of literature is not something to be confined within the walls of a classroom; a school of letters could exist in the community.

I communicated the idea to Benny, and he got together with two teachers, Prasad Master and his brother Pradeep, who had a key role in the running of the Readers' Forum at Alakode. Alakode is a place where the Marxist party, the Congress and the Kerala Congress held equal political strength, and so we decided right from the start that party political differences would be set aside in this space. We formed a syllabus including children's literature, short stories, novels, drama, literary theory, the contemporary relevance of literary writing, and reading. The classes were attended by over sixty people – farmers, rubber tappers, small-scale merchants, a few school students and teachers. Many of them had no preconceived notions or background in literature. And I found that, by the time we got to the end,

I could talk to them about Derrida, Foucault and high theory, and they were engaged.

The second Patashala was started in Madayi. Madayippara has become a familiar name among nature lovers in Kerala. It used to be over 660 acres, rich in natural diversity. In the distance, at one end of this expansive rocky area, is Ezhimala. This is a place of great natural beauty that instigates a sense of mental freedom. There is a small group here called 'Janakala Madayippara'. Janakala was very helpful, and here also I could conduct the Patashala very successfully, although the group was smaller with around thirty-five participants. In Alakode, they have continued the Patashala by organizing 'Veettumutta Sahitya Charcha' – literary discussions in the front yard.

So I believe that, in contemporary Kerala, if people are given opportunities to expand their skills to engage with literature and creative writing, it can make a huge impact on communication as well as mental well-being and intellectual abilities. I also believe that these are best organized independently, outside of the influence of party politics and organized sociocultural politics. You are aware, I am sure, of Azar Nafisi's book *The Republic of Imagination*. I guess we were trying to create a republic of imagination so that people can think beyond caste, religion and political leanings that inhibit real communication. I can tell you from my experience in Alakode and Madayi that this is possible.

JK: These are inspiring developments. Translation is also, in a sense, an attempt to expand the communication of ideas. When I started, I was quite surprised to find that not many of your works, apart from a previous translation of 'Pigman' and a few other stories, had been translated so far.

NP: True. 'Daivathinte Poombatta' (God's Butterfly) is one of my stories that has been received well in translation and has been translated into Urdu, Kannada, Telugu and English.

JK: Having worked on these stories, I believe that your work does not lend itself to a kind of straightforward translation, not that any translation is a simple, straightforward rendering into another language. I was very aware of the cultural specificity of the northern Kerala language, and the unique musicality within your very specific usage of it. The question was how to translate this without fetishizing it, without resorting to some kind of patois English. So my effort was to find a writing style that lends itself to preserving the uniqueness of your language while trying not to make it exotic. But I also think that it is not just a question of language and idiom. There is something about the stories that you tell that, even as they speak to a certain universality of experience, cling to the specificity of locale and context.

NP: I am not able to judge the translation from a perspective of English language proficiency. All I can say is that as far as I, the writer, is concerned, I felt that the translations captured the stories as I would have wanted them to be. As you said, it is not just a question of language. It is also culture – not just cultural references of specific words or metaphors, but the culture within which the characters and their lives are steeped. The success of the translation is based on the translator's ability to capture that. And I am pleased with what you have done with the stories.

JK: Thank you. 'Diary of a Malayali Madman' is the first story I worked on. I was in Kerala for an extended period after my father passed away. It is interesting that you talked about the culture of red tape that consumes our public offices, because I started translating the story, scribbling in a notebook, while spending endless hours in the waiting rooms and verandas of various government offices, trying to sort out his affairs. I finished the first draft really quickly. But this story is deceptively simple. It is only in the second and third reworking that the story and the characters – especially Aagi – reveal themselves. And that took several months. From my point of view as a translator, it has been a challenging but immensely pleasurable task. In terms of finding publishers, I think there are editors interested in regional language translations who are familiar with the northern Kerala milieu through the works of writers such as M. Mukundan. But your work opens up an entirely different world and writing style.

NP: I hope so. One of the issues writers of my generation have had to reckon with was the idea of modernity. The first story I wrote under the name N. Prabhakaran – I had been writing under another name for four or five years before that – was 'Ottayante Pappan' and that was in 1971. This was a time when modernity was being established in Malayalam literature. In some ways, it puts forth the philosophy of Existentialism which I talked about earlier. So in some of the writings at the time, there was an attempt to engage with existential issues without really having any experience of it and not knowing what existentialism as a philosophy means. There are many writers in my generation who felt that there was something fundamentally wrong with writing within a philosophical framework that one hasn't quite lived. But it was also a struggle to find ways of voicing things differently, because of the hegemony, in literary production, of modernity in the guise of versions of Existentialism – and it was difficult to overcome that hegemony. For example, N.S. Madhavan received the Mathrubhumi Prize for his short story 'Shishu' in 1970. My story came out in 1971. Madhavan had a long gap between his first anthology and his famous story 'Higuita' which he published in 1990. I too had such a gap. I published my first anthology in 1986, and when I was selecting stories for it, I realized that I had only eleven. I had been struggling to write and publish for almost fifteen years since 1971. It was only after that first anthology that I start making forays into other areas and ways of telling a story – both in form and content.

One of those new roads was leading me into folk traditions. The novel *Ezhinum Meethe* (Beyond Seven i.e. the mountain, specifically Kodagu mountain) is an example of this. I wrote this in 1985 and it came out in book form in 1986. It is the story of the folk-god Kathivanoor Veeran, and is written in the style and language of Thottam Pattu and the northern Malabar dialect. As you know, many of the stories told in the form of Theyyam are tragedies. And I find the story of Kathivanoor Veeran especially tragic. My attempt was to preserve this emotional content in the narration. More than anything else, it was an experiment in language. I think readers liked it, as it was quite different from anything I had written until then. It is my dream to rewrite this story, this time in more detail, engaging with the soci-ocultural context and history of Kodagu and north Kerala over three centuries. I have been working on this on and off for the last ten years, but it has been a slow process, inter-rupted by other engagements and pressures on my time.

JK: The interest in and influence of folklore and tradition is reflected in many of your other writings too, for example, the novella *Janthujanam* (Animal Folk), the play *Pulijanmam* (Born to be a Tiger) and the short story 'Daivathinte Poombatta'. Paralleling, and sort of interconnected to this, is the place that nature has in your work. This is evident in the descriptive passages as well as the real and metaphoric roles that elements of nature and its creatures – forests, trees and plants, animals, even the wind – take on. This deep connec-tion with nature – is it something that had always been there or something that has developed over time?

NP: I don't belong to any group bearing the label 'Nature Lovers'. In fact, I am not a good observer of nature. I feel nature. To be exact, I fall in love with some elements of nature. The primary school I attended was situated at the end of the northern slope of Madayippara, and the high school was also nearby. The greatest joy of my school days was wandering over Madayippara, in the Onam season for collecting flowers, and in the rest of the year to experience the various visual and sensory pleasures this vast expanse of rock, which changed its mood and expressions in accord-ance with the seasons, provided lavishly.

This intimate relationship with nature continued in a subdued manner even after my day-to-day connection became a memory. Wherever I go, I could easily sense the pulse of nature there, though details do not usually get registered in my mind. On many occasions, I ridiculed myself for not remembering things. But when I once again go through what I have written, I understand that nature – more than anything, an incomparable emotional truth – has come into my writing with utmost ease. For me, nature is not something to be objectively studied. I don't want to place myself outside nature and study it.

JK: Your non-human characters, for example, the protagonist in *Janthujanam*, the fox Chembankutty, is in many ways as embedded, observant and reflective a chronicler of local history and community as the human protagonists in your stories, especially the ones in this anthology.

NP: In some ways, a novelist is a historian. You know that Vaikom Muhammad Basheer has repeatedly used the term 'historian' to refer to the writer, the novelist, in his work. The Chinese writer, Mo Yan, for example, writes epic histories through his fiction. The novel is a sibling of history; a more lovable sibling.

JK: Yes. But I think I am making two distinctions here. First, I'd argue that, beyond the writer, your protagonists themselves take on the work of the historian. History, then, is the telling of the mundane, everyday life. And second, this is different from historical fiction, which I see as having a different purpose.

NP: I agree. Yiddish writer Isaac Bashevis Singer, for example, is writing about local people and local history, while his protagonists do the work of historicizing the Jewish life of a period. I admire writers like him and Ngūgī wa Thiong'o who use symbolism and magic realism as forms of history-writing. In *Wizard of the Crow*, the Free Republic of Aburīria is as real as any country of our age in the Global South. The story becomes history. I believe that there comes a point in the narration of the life history of a region when history and fiction come together to become inseparable, where it becomes difficult to say where fiction ends and history begins. I do believe that it can be almost a more authentic history, as long as the writer goes beyond the written, recorded, 'authenticated' histories and actively looks for historical knowledge located elsewhere, in memory and lore, and beyond his own imagined worlds into a genuine eagerness and interest in historical inquiry. I am adapted to this line. I try actively to find a balance between magic realism, realism and hyperrealism keeping in mind that my prime motive is to reach the core of a reality.

For my novel *Janakatha* (Peoples' Story), I interviewed many men and women of the villages in and around Ezhimala and Madayi. The data I could gather from the interviews, I used freely. I think that the whole novel is a sort of local history reconstructed, giving ample space for imagination. If you do not insist upon specific dates and matter-of-fact descriptions of incidents, you can read it as the social and cultural history of the region in the twentieth century. I attach more importance to the fact that I could capture what I believe is the mental world of ordinary men and women who are usually denied entry into history.

In my current writing, as I said at the start, I am trying something else too, and that is to leave the writing free, free-flowing, with minimal editing – both ideological editing, and aesthetic editing that is concerned with formal structures or beauty of writing. I am eager to see where this process will take me. It definitely energizes me. It is a continuation of the move beyond the influence of modernism and revolutionary left-wing politics and Marxist philosophy that had characterized the writers of my generation, including myself. A move, even, beyond the complex discussions about a writer's social responsibility and legitimacy. These are important considerations, but I do also feel the need to move beyond these in my writings. I would like to say that literature is nothing but freedom – freedom from all preconceived notions.

Acknowledgments

Reading the translations of my stories included in this book, I marvel at the impulse that made me write them. They got written at various points. I am using the passive voice here because, as I read through the translations, I was struck by the notion that, beyond any conscious decisions and planning on my part, the form and content of these stories have taken on a life of their own. Perhaps translation allows a writer to consider possibilities in his writing that he hasn't considered before.

I have tried to look at the lives around me from close proximity, without getting bogged down in the details of their material contexts. My effort has been to find ways of recording the workings of their minds in the forms and language they demand. I feel proud that, rather than reconstructing other lives from my imagination, I was able to immerse myself in their inherent truths, stripping myself of preconceived notions about life and art. Will my readers agree with this claim? This is not a consideration I agonize over.

It was entirely unexpectedly that Jayasree Kalathil, then a complete stranger to me, came up with the idea of translating these stories. The simplicity and grace of these translations has convinced me that it was good I didn't feel the need to ponder over it before making a decision. My gratitude to Jayasree, and to the publishers.

– N. Prabhakaran

I read the small paperback edition of 'Oru Malayali Bhranthante Diary' (Diary of a Malayali Madman) at a difficult time in my life, following the death of my father. Translating the book gave me something to do as I brooded over my difficult and complex relationship with him, which, on reflection, was also exquisitely ordinary. Soon, the idea of a translated collection of stories by the master narrator of the extraordinary in the ordinary in Malayalam literature took root. I am grateful to N. Prabhakaran for trusting me with this, and for working with me to finalize the selection, for the gentle and careful feedback on each draft, and for allowing me glimpses into his creative process.

I am also grateful to our editor, Rahul Soni, who embraced the project right from my first – unsolicited – email about it, to Tejaswini Niranjana for putting me in touch with him, and to Adley Siddiqi, Alison Faulkner, R. Srivatsan and Susie Tharu for reading early drafts.

– Jayasree Kalathil

N Prabhakaran is a major contemporary writer in Kerala and is considered a pioneer of the post-modern aesthetic turn in Malayalam literature. He has published over forty works of novels, poetry, plays, short story collections, essays and a memoir. He is the recipient of several honours including the Kerala Sahitya Akademi award; the EMS Memorial Trust Award; the Vaikom Muhammed Basheer Memorial Trust award; the Malayatoor Award; and the Muttathu Varky Literary Award for Contributions to Malayalam literature. *Diary of a Malayali Madman*, translated by Jayasree Kalathil, won the 2019 Crossword Book Award. His latest novel, *Mayamanushyar*, won the Odakkuzhal Award in 2020.

Jayasree Kalathil's translations have won the JCB Prize for Literature (for S. Hareesh's *Moustache* in 2020) and the Crossword Book Award (for N. Prabhakaran's *Diary of a Malayali Madman* in 2019). Her latest translation, Sheela Tomy's *Valli*, was shortlisted for the 2022 JCB Prize for Literature and for the Atta Galatta-BLF Book Prize. She is the author of the children's book *The Sackclothman*, which has been translated into Malayalam, Telugu and Hindi. She was selected as one of the two translators-in-residence at the British Centre for Literary Translation, University of East Anglia, in 2023.

PARTNERS

pixel ||| texel

ADDITIONAL DONORS, CONT'D

Mike Soto
Mokhtar Ramadan
Nikki & Dennis Gibson
Patrick Kukucka
Patrick Kutcher
Rev. Elizabeth & Neil Moseley
Richard Meyer
Scott & Katy Nimmons
Sherry Perry

Sydneyann Binion
Stephen Harding
Stephen Williamson
Susan Carp
Susan Ernst
Theater Jones
Tim Perttula
Tony Thomson

SUBSCRIBERS

Caroline West
Elizabeth Simpson
Nicole Yurcaba
Jennifer Owen
Melanie Nicholls
Alan Glazer
Matt Bucher
Katarzyna Bartoszynska
Michael Binkley
Erin Kubatzky
Michael Lighty
Joseph Rebella
Jarratt Willis
Heustis Whiteside
Samuel Herrera
Josh Rubenoff
Reid Sharpless
Damon Copeland
Kyle Trimmer
Kenneth McClain

Scott Chiddister
Ryan Todd
Petra Hendrickson
Austin Dearborn
Hillary Richards
Nancy Keaton
Nancy Allen
John Mitchell
Sian Valvis
Jessica Sirs
Courtney Sheedy
John Andrew Margrave
John Tenny
Dauphin Ewart
Heath Dollar
Conner Cunningham
Tom Bowden
Margaret Terwey
Jona Gerlach
Sabrina Balgamwalla Harriman

Whitney O Banner
Jeffrey Nichols
Hannah Good
Ashley Cline
Vee Kalkunte
Connor Shirley
Jack Waters
Stephen Fuller
Kirsten Murchison
Jennifer Caroll
Agi Bori Mottern
Margaret Cochran
Crystal Cardenas
Alina Stefanescu Coryell
Kate Sherrod
Angela Schlegel
Michael Peirson
Marya Hart
Carole Hailey

AVAILABLE NOW FROM DEEP VELLUM